# MR. BLUE

Also by

Myles Connolly

*The Bump on Brannigan's Head*

*Dan England and the Noonday Devil*

*The Reason for Ann*

*Three Who Ventured*

# MR. BLUE

Myles Connolly

*With an Introduction and Notes by*
Stephen Mirarchi, Ph.D.

&

*A Preface by*
Mary Connolly Breiner

CLUNY MEDIA

Cluny Media edition, 2015

This Cluny edition includes minor editorial revisions to the original text.

Cluny Media edition copyright © 1956 by Myles Connolly;
reprinted by permission.

ISBN: 9781944418076

Cover design by Clarke & Clarke
Cover image: Childe Hassam, *Fifth Avenue*,
oil on canvas, 1919
Courtesy of Wikimedia Commons

*To Agnes Bevington*

# Contents

# Preface

When I was asked to write a preface for this new edition of *Mr. Blue*, I was filled with so many loving thoughts and memories of Mr. Blue's amazing 88-year odyssey, from the first edition in 1928 to this first version available as an eBook so many decades later.

I remember my father's words, in the preface for the first paperback edition in 1954, when he pointed out that Mr. Blue had walked into a very old world in 1928. It was a world where the mechanists and pragmatists ruled science and philosophy "with an austerely and authoritarian withering hand." In religion, he noted "the rationalist theologians were boldly and coldly reducing the strangeness and wonders of religious faith to logic. Wisdom was little more than a rumor. And there was a new, dull faith that only knowledge mattered."

This was not a world that was going to welcome Mr. Blue, the essence of youth, "believing ardently in the joy of living that belongs to the pure in heart and the laughter that comes from innocence surprised."

To be sure, Mr. Blue's first steps into the world were tentative. The novel sold only 70 copies one year! But then gradually, miraculously, everything changed.

Sales began to increase. The book was published in England, Brazil, Germany, Italy, and the Netherlands, enrapturing ever-growing numbers of readers while some of the bestsellers of 1928 slid into oblivion.

My father was delighted and a bit puzzled as *Mr. Blue* evolved over the decades from its shaky start to dancing into the hearts and minds of people around the world. He wondered if its growing success might be due to something in Mr. Blue's particular philosophy that has become more acceptable, more embraceable, in recent years.

"Could it be that the world has grown younger? Wiser? Happier?" he asked. "Could it be that Christians aren't making such a secret of their joy as they once did?"

Joy in living one's faith is the heart of Mr. Blue's philosophy. According to my father, "Mr. Blue would have died rather than accept that the glory of life could be weighed and measured and codified, that the wonders of religious faith could be filed away in neat little categories by logic and reason."

Indeed, Mr. Blue worried, back in the 1920s, about how young people would keep their faith in an imagined time, a century into the future, when the world might be indifferent to faith and beset with religious intolerance.

We're fast approaching that century mark and, in some ways, Mr. Blue's words seem prophetic as indifference to faith and religious intolerance make headlines these days. And yet…there are so many signs of hope and so many reasons to rejoice.

Pope Francis speaks ardently to us about the virtues of charity and compassion, about mercy and sharing of the joy and wonder of faith. These are the very virtues that Mr. Blue embodies! I have a feeling that Pope Francis would like Mr. Blue, that they would be true brothers in spirit.

And were my father here to see all that has happened in Mr. Blue's odyssey, I imagine that he would be both humbled and pleased to see that Mr. Blue is as relevant today as he was when he first stepped out into the world all those years ago to tell a timeless story about celebrating the glorious intangibles of life.

*~Mary Connolly Breiner*
*February 26, 2016*

# Introduction

*Nota bene*: Both parts of this introduction refer freely to the events of *Mr. Blue*, including its ending. First-time readers may wish to skip directly to the novel and return here afterwards.

## I. A Brief History of *Mr. Blue*

When Macmillan first published *Mr. Blue* in 1928, it went largely unnoticed. The few reviewers of the book found the title character "dull and false," with religious critics in particular judging him "an imposter and a bore" (Connolly 9). A review in *The Irish Monthly* in early 1930 absolved author Myles Connolly of his literary sin, for Blue "has lived, loved life, and said so many beautiful, though inspiring, things that one can forgive the author for creating him" (55).

Even if *Mr. Blue* had been overlooked by many, it became "a popular item among Catholic collegians in the 1930s" (Sparr 193). Connolly's reputation grew, and his status as a "man of letters" was secure enough that the *Mark Twain Quarterly* consulted him in 1939 for one of their "G. K. C. and American Authors" articles, which explored the influence of G. K. Chesterton among the bright lights of American writers. "The stuff of immortality was so strong in him that beside his memory as the world calls it, it is we who are dead," responded Connolly in his admiration of Chesterton. "Writing was life with him: it was his breathing, his talk, his laughter, his self" (12).

Sales of *Mr. Blue* steadily increased in the 1940s. In a 1951 interview with *The Pilot*, the newspaper of the Catholic Archdiocese of Boston, Connolly revealed his reasons for producing fiction: "I am not interested in writing bestsellers…I am primarily interested in entertaining people and telling them a fundamental truth at the same time and telling them in a hearty, wholesome way—through laughter" (9). Yet by the mid-1950s, the paperback edition released by Image Books proudly proclaimed on its cover, "Over one half million copies sold." In his 1954 introduction to the silver anniversary edition of *Mr. Blue*, Connolly expressed his wonder and surprise at how the book had become a hit. Mr. Blue, the character, "was making more friends here and abroad than he had in any year in the previous twenty-five," and Connolly, with his ready wit, acknowledged that "certainly, I had nothing to do with it" (10).

Connolly died ten years after writing the silver anniversary preface—July 15, 1964—and merited an obituary in *The New York Times*. He had built such a name for himself as a Hollywood screenwriter and producer that those credits took prominence in the notice. A few paragraphs down, however, was this very telling tribute: "*Mr. Blue...* has been reprinted numerous times and also has been published in England and Brazil. The story of Mr. Blue, described as a modern St. Francis, has been required reading in many colleges and high schools in the United States" (27).

Amidst the post-Vatican II shakeups, however, *Mr. Blue* began to decline. By the early 1970s it had a small yet loyal fan base; it was a cult book, a "little underground classic" according to Jesuit historian Raymond Schroth (79). Writing in 1972, Schroth called for a recovery "of the creative spirit in the American church" and highlighted many overlooked books that ought to be reread, including two works of fiction—one of them *Mr. Blue* (78). "Fiction has been more ready to stand against our culture" than religious political writing, he asserted, and Connolly's novel "defied our 1920s gluttony with the unrealistic madness of Franciscan love" (79).

A few years later, a substantial piece on the direction of Catholic fiction—aptly titled "Since Blue Died"—ran in *The Critic*, the journal of the Thomas More Association. Jesuit author Michael Quillin opened the article with a seeming requiem for *Mr. Blue* and its hero: "The novel has not really been replaced with another, more contemporary vision of the Catholic in the world. No one figure from literature dominates in the same fashion, possibly because the reality is no longer so monolithic" (25). Quillin then explored up-and-coming works by promising authors—including one Walker Percy—making the implicit point that to understand the great Catholic fiction of the past, one need be familiar with Blue.

The advice seems to have gone unheeded. Sometime in the 1980s *Mr. Blue* "went out of print...lost in the post-Vatican II shuffle" (Finley

6). One writer was able to buy a paperback directly from the publisher in 1987 but couldn't secure a second; "I may have bought the last copy of *Mr. Blue*," he lamented (Clark).

Many critics of this time agreed with Connolly—all too readily—that he had little to do with his own success. Historian James Fisher argued that the popularity of *Mr. Blue* could be traced to the rise of the Catholic Worker movement in the 1930s and 1940s as exemplified in Dorothy Day, the anti-establishment servant of the poor (Fisher 96). *Mr. Blue* was one of the "two most important works of Catholic fiction from the era" because "this new Catholic temperament" of radical generosity to the lowest of the low legitimated the book. In the words of Jesuit John Breslin, "[Blue] was a mystical type who combined the social activism of Dorothy Day with the contemplative reserve of Thomas Merton. In short, he made Catholicism cool" ("Jean Sulivan" 27). Fisher didn't think much of the book, though, in terms of literary merit. Even though Connolly was a clever craftsman, "*Mr. Blue* is an exceedingly grim and melancholy work. The hero…is sexless, rootless, and ageless" (97).

A nostalgic essay in a late 1980s edition of *Commonweal* went further. Reflecting on the first

time she read *Mr. Blue* in the late 1960s, Kathy
Cecala admitted that Connolly's book was merely
one among many: "I wish I could report that J. Blue
changed my life, skewed it in a crazy, colorful, and
profoundly altruistic direction" (590). Rereading
the novel, she found herself "strongly identifying
this time with the book's narrator...Blue, for all
his holy speeches and ultimate act of charity—
giving up his life to save another's—seemed a little
self-absorbed, turned inward" (591).

Appearing just after these evaluations was
a comprehensively researched article in an
early 1989 edition of the *St. Petersburg Times*.
Interviewing the high school teacher who had
taught him *Mr. Blue* more than two decades
earlier as well as Connolly's surviving children,
Roy Peter Clark shed much light on Connolly's
fiery yet compassionate personality, his near-mad
dedication to his principles, and his ardent love
of Catholicism. His allegiance to his faith was
matched only by his appetite for books, too many
of which almost ruined his marriage, joked Clark.

His love of writing had started early, Clark
discovered. Connolly had already imbibed deeply
of Chesterton by 1918, as a piece in the Boston
College literary publication *The Stylus*, which
Connolly edited that year, evinced: "St. Francis

of Assisi sang as he died. Chesterton would have Christ smiling at our foibles. By all means let us make a Spring resolution: When everything goes wrong we shall whistle" (quoted in Clark). Always pursuing freedom for excellence, Connolly managed as editor of the internationally distributed Knights of Columbus magazine *Columbia* in the mid-1920s to get Chesterton himself, as well as his prominent friend Hilaire Belloc, to contribute even more articles (Clark, Pelowski). A daily Mass-goer, Connolly not only held firmly to his beliefs when working in Hollywood but encouraged others to pursue the truth—including Frank Capra, star director of *Mr. Smith Goes to Washington* (1939) and *It's a Wonderful Life* (1946). In his autobiography, Capra called him "my great friend and critic...our relationship was a hate-love affair. We were either embracing or snarling...Connolly hurt because he was right" (121, 122). Capra would attend Connolly's funeral; his "grief when Connolly died...was intense" (McBride 222).

Rereading *Mr. Blue* was far from a disappointment for Clark: "The story came rushing back...[Blue] was completely in the world, but not of it...He was white and Catholic but hung out with blacks and Jews...He was a clown, a good Samaritan, a mystic, a theologian, a saint, a pilgrim and finally, a martyr. People who met him, or read about him, were changed forever." Connolly's daughter Mary kept the book in mind, as well: "As I grew up, I remembered things about Blue's character, the love for people, all minorities…It was sort of ahead of its time" (Clark). Contemplating *Mr. Blue*'s ending, Clark closed the feature hoping that many others would meet Blue in "libraries and in used book stores."

In response, a small press by the name of Richelieu Court Publications reprinted the novel in 1990—in hardcover, to boot. *Our Sunday Visitor* celebrated the occasion with a full-page article, complete with a beach house photo of a dashing Connolly. The *OSV* article was overwhelmingly positive in lauding Connolly's profound spiritual vision: "Deep, deep, deep down along the hidden pathways of the human heart, there is a place that only God can find—God, and once in a century or so, one of God's storytellers. Such a one was Myles Connolly, and such a story is *Mr. Blue*." The *OSV* author did express some reservations: "Connolly's 'negroes' are one racial stereotype piled on top of another," and "at times, Connolly's theology constitutes a period piece, too" (Finley 6).

The Richelieu Court edition was not

long-lived, but it evoked memories. In 2002, Breslin published an in-depth piece on the novel in *Boston College Magazine*, seeing Chesterton and Connolly as kindred spirits. Through his works, Chesterton "threw open doors and windows in a Church that seemed cautious to a fault and not very interested in new ideas…[he] made orthodoxy exciting, even dangerous." Enter Connolly's Blue, a knife-edge dancer of orthodoxy, "its ardent embodiment." Breslin speculated that Connolly, "as well read" as he was, offered *Mr. Blue* at least in part as a riposte to F. Scott Fitzgerald's *The Great Gatsby*, which had been published only three years earlier. While Gatsby "finds himself defeated by…mammon and his memory of Daisy," Blue declares and celebrates "a Christianity full of romance and gusto." While Fitzgerald gets lost in the past, Connolly gives us the appeal of "a uniquely American personality."

Chet Raymo had a very different reaction. In a short piece for the journal *Spiritus*, he remembered reading *Mr. Blue* in the 1950s; its success led "several generations of young Catholics to find more in their faith than formulaic prayers and rote dogma" (231). Nearly fifty years later in 2003, he reread it: "My first impression was surprise that I could ever have been inspired by a book that is so slight, so trite, so without literary merit…His book is a compendium of platitudes, and his character Blue now seems somewhat of an insufferable prig, who thought most of his fellow human beings had as little capacity for life as cabbages" (Raymo 232). Taking stock of his first impression, Raymo continued: "There is something to be said for moderation, especially in a world wracked by religious strife and by the hypocrisy and arrogance of institutional churches…If you wish, call the place I am at mediocrity. I am happy to live there without the company of Blue" (Raymo 233).

Loyola Classics picked up *Mr. Blue* in 2005. James Martin, the Jesuit priest of *My Life with the Saints* fame, wrote a brief piece in *America* announcing the good news—and that he had chosen it for discussion "in a book club at a local Jesuit parish" (2). A review in the *National Catholic Reporter* occasioned by Loyola's reprinting was comparable to earlier estimations in that it held up the book for its counter-cultural weight yet downplayed its status as literature. According to the *NCR* author, *Mr. Blue* was to be praised for "its cinematic flavor and vivid descriptions of color and urban scenery," but the novel was "not a great work of art" (Linner 4a). The great spiritual value of the book was how the protagonist "in embracing his cross...leaves the logic of the world while remaining a witness to it."

Interest in *Mr. Blue* and Connolly continued to build. A major new book on Capra appeared in 2011, with biographer Joseph McBride writing that the director "greatly admired" *Mr. Blue* and that "it was a seminal, though largely unrecognized, source of ideas Capra would adopt in his films" (221). Jesuit George Drance staged a one-hour "dramatic reading" of *Mr. Blue*, based on a script by playwright Mary Kay Williams, in the heart of Manhattan in early 2014, expanding and elaborating on it in 2015 (Tueth, Pelowski). Mary, Connolly's daughter, attended both. *Columbia* ran a feature on Connolly in its June 2014 issue, including an excerpt of an unpublished column Connolly wrote before retiring as editor of that same magazine nearly ninety years earlier (Pelowski). In their Christmas 2014 issue, *Catholic Insight* printed a seven-page excerpt from Connolly's *Dan England and the Noonday Devil* (1951) in their Literary Digressions section. Appropriately, a reprint of Chesterton's essay "The Modern Scrooge" followed.

Loyola Classics pared down their offerings in 2015, and—once again—*Mr. Blue* was out of print.

## II. Literary Technique in *Mr. Blue*

As the Notes at the end of this volume attest, Connolly deserves more merit as an author of fiction than he has been afforded. Within a narrative of two friends' helping each other to live their vocations, Connolly deftly weaves architectural, regional, theological, Scriptural, literary, liturgical, and historical threads that enrich the story with interdisciplinary magnitude. Obviously in control of his craft, Connolly "plays" within the framework he sets up, riffing on words' double meanings and alluding to authors like Chesterton with joyful significance.

The overall structure of *Mr. Blue* has long been overlooked, probably because it is so simple, and yet its simplicity is crucial for understanding the work and not misinterpreting it. As mentioned earlier, there is ample evidence to suggest that Connolly saw his novel as a response to Fitzgerald's *The Great Gatsby*. Several weeks before his novel was printed, Fitzgerald, who was "never satisfied" with the title, wanted to change it to *Under the Red White and Blue* (207). Such a title would presumably provoke readers into contemplating the book's events as a lament on what had happened to the American dream. The overall trajectory of Gatsby's character in the book, in fact, follows the sequence of an inverted flag: blue, white, and red.

Gatsby begins the novel with the blues, "trying to forget something very sad that had happened," and Nick comes to realize his loss of Daisy as the source of "the gnawings of his broken heart" (70, 71). Daisy shares in this sadness: when she and Gatsby meet again for the first time in nearly five years, Nick describes her voice as "full of aching, grieving beauty [that] told only of her unexpected joy" (94). A little while later in Gatsby's house, she "[begins] to cry stormily" when she sees Gatsby's wealth, represented by his gorgeous shirts (98). As the two begin an adulterous affair, their blues turn to a kind of wedding white, with Gatsby firing his servants to prevent gossip (120). With an actual wedding occurring in the ballroom below them, Gatsby asks Daisy to deny her past and join him. She balks, however, and despite seeing an apparent reconciliation between Daisy and her husband Tom while staked out in the couple's bushes, Gatsby waits for a follow-up phone call from her and covers up the evidence that she killed Tom's mistress while driving. Fitzgerald depicts this waiting period as a self-proclaimed martyr's complex: Gatsby carries on his shoulders a false cross (a "pneumatic mattress") to his pool—his place of death—stumbling along the way, and his assassin shoots out of ignorance, having assumed that Gatsby was driving the car that killed his wife, Tom's mistress (169). Gatsby's cross-mattress floats on an "accidental course with its accidental burden...a thin red circle in the water" (170). From blue to white to red—the American dream inverted, ruined, by the restlessness of the denizens of the Jazz Age, with Gatsby its false savior.

Connolly structured his book in the same progression—blue, white, and red—but with these stages representing spiritual growth, not further dissolution. That color progression as related to the path to God is a mainstay of Irish Catholic spirituality, and Connolly was well read in the literature of his Irish heritage. The seventh-century *Cambrai Homily*—a monument in historical studies as the earliest Irish homily—contains, in addition to the expected Latin, passages written in Old Irish that speak of a threefold martyrdom: white, blue, and red. While the middle color, blue, is sometimes rendered as green depending on the translation, Charles D. Wright, scholar of Celtic and Anglo-Saxon literature, notes that the white, blue, and red pattern is "a distinction by color that occurs in a variety of Irish and Hiberno-Latin texts" (Wright 74).

A literal translation of the *Cambrai Homily* tells when a person is living each color of the threefold martyrdom. He is white, "when he separates for sake of God everything he loves, although he suffer fasting or labor thereat"; blue, "when by means of them (fasting and labor) he separates from his desires, or suffers toil in penance and repentance"; and red, "endurance of a cross or destruction for Christ's sake" (Stokes 247). In modern terms, says Orthodox theologian Kallistos Ware, blue is "'to free oneself from evil desires by means of fasting and labor,' pursuing the ascetic way in one's homeland"; white, "to 'abandon everything one loves for God's sake,' that is, to accept the vocation of wandering, pilgrimage, voluntary exile for Christ;" and "red martyrdom is to shed one's blood for Christ" (Ware 122).

Such is the title character's journey in *Mr. Blue*. Happy when he meets the narrator, Blue indeed pursues generosity and fasting in his homeland, but he is not quite fulfilled, as he has yet to embrace fully his life's vocation. He finds greater inspiration in giving of himself to others like the priest White, exercising his "common" or "baptismal priesthood" based on White's sacramental priesthood as he takes up the cause of pilgrimage to the lumberyards (*Catechism* §§1546–47). At the end of the book, Blue freely gives his life for another, meriting the Red. Blue lives the *Cambrai Homily* in the particular, concrete circumstances of his life, and the narrator, in the writing of the book, is beginning to do the same.

Connolly has thus achieved the rather impressive feat of bringing his characters through a time-honored Catholic spiritual transformation to the perfection of love while using that same pattern to refute the very structure of the book he considered most deserving of counterpoint. Fitzgerald, a lapsed Catholic, uses blue, white, and red to point to the inversion, the decline, and even the degeneration of the American dream. Connolly's blue, white, and red bring the reader the glory of the ancient Irish-Catholic spiritual tradition and reinvigorate the American national dream by integrating it with God's dream for each of his creatures: the perfection of charity according to the gifts and circumstances of each.

Through literature, Connolly was in his time upholding and strengthening the growth of the Catholic Church in America, specifically through his heritage. As historian Charles R. Morris observes of the Church in the early 1900s, "Just as Catholicism came to define much of what it was to be Irish, America became Ireland's 'second fatherland'" (111). In Connolly's time, the archbishops—and eventually cardinals—of Boston, Philadelphia, and New York were all Irish-Americans, all "centralizers, standardizers, and disciplinarians" (115). Faithful and patriotic as he was, Connolly would not stand by and let Fitzgerald pronounce both the American dream and Catholicism dead in the water.

It is no coincidence, for example, that as the narrator and Blue journey from the pre-Revolutionary oyster house in downtown Boston to Copley Square, Connolly brings them past the great sites and centers of the American Revolution, including the balcony where the Declaration was first proclaimed. At the end of this sojourn, Blue lets the narrator know that he's taking up his cross; he's beginning his journey into White territory—a wandering to the poorest of the city. Connolly has brought us through a kind of *via crucis*, a way of the cross, impregnated with the spirit of the American Revolution. To be a spiritual warrior of the highest caliber is to embrace the spirit of free and total self-offering, the true patriotism Chesterton speaks of that revolutionizes not only nations but souls themselves.

Understanding Connolly's literary-spiritual structure clears away many obstacles critics have presented over the years. There is no need, for instance, to "take sides" with Blue or the narrator, for both are moving through their blue and white stages, albeit one more quickly than the other. As the *Cambrai Homily* implies, the red will not be asked of all, but the white will, for it represents the complete freedom from attachment to all creatures—anything not the Creator—for love of God. Other Catholic sources, in fact, have seen the red and white martyrdoms as two sides of the same sacrifice. Third-century Church Father St. Cyprian of Carthage, for instance, distinguishes "the red martyrdom of blood in times of persecution [from] the white martyrdom of self-sacrificing compassion and acts of charity in times of peace" (Ware 121–22).

Connolly has a final literary trick up his sleeve that brings this spiritual battle directly to the reader. When the narrator returns to see him in the hospital, Blue has died suddenly, and another visitor has preceded the narrator: the owner of the car that struck Blue. Shaking his head disdainfully, the owner jumps to conclusions about who Blue is based on his association with the poor and implies that he got what he deserved. The narrator is dumbstruck, and the narrative abruptly shifts two years forward to the present. In this moment, readers have several choices: they can condemn the owner, vent some anger at him, maybe even on some secret level agree with him—until they realize that the owner, too, is someone Blue has died for.

Do readers dare forgive him, this reckless, haughty driver; might they will his good, as Blue himself even encouraged: "Did you ever try to love someone who was mean, petty, shallow, selfish? Try it" (77)? Connolly offers us this chance to embrace Blue's mission in an intimate way, and whether we assent is up to us.

The narrator assents, for the inveterate skepticism he had leveled against Blue's life he now directs at Blue's death: "No one so brave, so heroic, so glorious…can leave us suddenly like that" (125). His pragmatism is now properly ordered, for what could be more practical than getting out the word about Blue? In writing the book, the narrator embraces the pilgrimage, the mission, of the white martyrdom and begins exercising more fully his common priesthood according to his particular gifts.

If readers sense the joyful call to do the same, then Connolly's literary gem will have been all the more successful in imparting the "practical wisdom" of great art (*Catechism* §2501). They will become, as Connolly himself said, "more aware of the strange and tender God who by His birth and life and death has given individual birth and life and death, no matter how obscure and drab and common, a radiant and prevailing glory and an everlasting importance" (11).

> ~*Stephen Mirarchi,*
> *Atchison, Kansas*
> *January 29, 2016*

Stephen Mirarchi (Ph.D., Brandeis University) is Assistant Professor of English at Benedictine College in Atchison, Kansas. His articles have appeared in journals like *The Edgar Allan Poe Review*, *Christianity & Literature*, *Religion & the Arts*, *Homiletic and Pastoral Review*, and *Dappled Things*; in a critical edition of Stephen Crane's *The Red Badge of Courage*; and in magazines and newspapers like *The Boston Globe*, *The National Catholic Register*, *Crisis*, and others.

# Bibliography

Breslin, John. "The Improbable Career of Mr. Blue." *Boston College Magazine* (Winter 2002). Web. 25 March 2015.

____. "Jean Sulivan (1913-80): Rebel Prophet of God's Kingdom." *America* 183:8 (23 September 2000): 27. *General OneFile*. Web. 23 June 2015.

Capra, Frank. *The Name Above the Title: An Autobiography*. 1971. Boston: Da Capo Press, 1997. Print.

Carty, Walter V. "Myles Connolly Sings in His Books the 'Adventure of Catholicism.'" *The Pilot* (8 December 1951): 9. Print.

*Catechism of the Catholic Church*. 2nd ed. Rome: Libreria Editrice Vaticana, 1997. Print.

Cecala, Kathy Petersen. "Does anyone remember J. Blue?" *Commonweal* 115:19 (4 November 1988): 590-91. Print.

Clark, Roy Peter. "Mystery in Blue." *St. Petersburg*

*Times* (28 January 1989): 4E. *ProQuest Central.* Web. 30 November 2015.

Connolly, Myles. "Introduction." *Mr. Blue.* 1928. Garden City, NY: Image Books, 1954. Print.

Finley, Mitch. "'Mr. Blue': a kite-flying prophet of a living faith." *Our Sunday Visitor* 79 (22 July 1990): 6. *ATLA Catholic Periodical and Literature Index.* 23 June 2015.

Fisher, James Terence. *The Catholic Counterculture in America, 1933–1962.* Chapel Hill: University of North Carolina Press, 1989. Print.

Fitzgerald, F. Scott. *The Great Gatsby: The Authorized Text.* 1925. (New York: Scribner, 1995). Print.

"G. K. C. and American Authors: Part Two." *Mark Twain Quarterly* 3:3 (Summer-Fall 1939): 11-13. *JSTOR.* Web. 4 September 2015.

Linner, Rachelle. "Meeting Mr. Blue." *National Catholic Reporter* (20 May 2005): 4a. *Academic OneFile.* Web. 23 June 2015.

Martin, James. "Of many things." *America* 193:14 (7 November 2005): 2. *Academic OneFile.* Web. 23 June 2015.

McBride, Joseph. *Frank Capra: The Catastrophe of Success.* Jackson: University of Mississippi Press, 2011. *eBook Collection (EBSCOhost).* Web. 25 March 2015.

Morris, Charles R. *American Catholic: The Saints and Sinners Who Built America's Most Powerful Church.* 1997. New York: Vintage, 1998. Print.

"Myles Connolly, a Film Writer, 66." *New York Times* (17 July 1964): 27. Microfilm.

"Myles Connolly, Dan England and the Noonday Devil." *Catholic Insight* (December 2014): 13-15. *Gale PowerSearch.* Web. 23 June 2015.

Pelowski, Alton J. "Remembering Mr. Blue." *Columbia* (1 June 2014). Web. 25 January 2016.

Quillin, Michael. "Since Blue Died: American Catholic Novels Since 1961." *The Critic* 34 (Fall 1975): 25-35. Print.

Raymo, Chet. "Mr. Blue Redux." *Spiritus* 3:2 (Fall 2003): 231-33. *ATLA Religion Database with ATLASerials.* 23 June 2015.

Rev. of *Mr. Blue*, by Myles Connolly. *The Irish Monthly* 58:679 (January 1930): 55. *JSTOR.* Web. 4 July 2015.

Schroth, Raymond A. "Recovering American Catholic Culture." *New Catholic World* 215:1283 (March/April 1972): 78-9. Print.

Sparr, Arnold. *To Promote, Defend, and Redeem: The Catholic Literary Revival and the Cultural Transformation of American Catholicism, 1920–1960.* New York: Greenwood Press, 1990. Print.

Stokes, Whitley and John Strachan, eds. *Thesaurus Palaeohibernicus*, volume II. Cambridge: Cambridge University Press, 1903. Print.

Tueth, Michael V. "A Journey with 'Mr. Blue.'" *America* (29 May 2014). Web. 25 March 2015.

Ware, Kallistos. *The Inner Kingdom.* Crestwood, New York: St. Vladimir's Seminary Press,

2000. Print.

Wright, Charles D. *The Irish Tradition in Old English Literature.* Cambridge: Cambridge University Press, 1993. Print.

# Acknowledgements

The writer of the Introduction and Notes would like to thank the Forsyth Library at the Fort Hays State University in Hays, Kansas, for their generous loaning of Hilary Pepler's *Pertinent & Impertinent*, of which only 200 copies were printed in 1926, and of which only forty-two are housed in libraries worldwide. He offers a hearty thank-you to Alton Pelowski, who generously provided a copy of the 1951 *Boston Pilot* interview. He would also like to thank Christopher Childers, Assistant Professor of History at Benedictine College in Atchison, Kansas, for his assistance in looking over the Introduction and Notes, and for his helpful suggestions thereof.

# Foreword

I give here briefly and roughly a few episodes from the latter years of J. Blue. Mr. Blue was a unique figure in American life. It is a pity his story is so little known. I hope this contribution will lead those who knew him better, especially in his earlier days, to add their bit to a fitting and useful monument to his memory.

Some years ago it was written of Mr. Blue:

> It is impossible to be with him an hour without breathing a new wholesome air, charged with beauty. It is impossible to be with him and not catch the spectacular glory of the present moment. At the power of his presence, before the eloquence of

his eyes, poverty, neglect, and such trifles become as nothing. One feels bathed in a brilliant and even tangible light, for it is the light he sees, and which, he would have us believe, is about us on our gallant journey toward death. All the scales of pettiness fall off the soul. The spirit stands up, clean, shining, valiant, in an unconscious effort to match his. But then he is gone, with his tears and laughter and his dazzling glory. "Come, come," his eyes say. "Behold the perilous road!" No one follows, I believe. And sometimes I wonder if he cares. "You will die, stifled with comfortability and normality, choked by small joys and small sorrows." Such is his warning as he goes. What can a man do with a fellow like that?

This passage caught the spirit of his life very well. But no writing could catch the splendor of his adventures. Let not the critical think that I have tried to do so in this book.

# Chapter 1

I had not heard from Blue for a year. He had written me from England where he had gone on a pilgrimage to Tyburn and the places of Thomas More. He had written something about generosity or humor. I had written back, urging him to get a good job with a reliable firm or he would end up in the poorhouse. "That will be glorious," he replied. "I have long known the magnificent possibilities of living in a poorhouse. I will become the troubadour of the poorhouse."

I have not the slightest doubt he would have been, in spite of his youth (he was not yet thirty), immensely happy in a poorhouse. He had no money. When by accident he happened upon some he gave it away. He worked here and there for his meals and a place to sleep. He roamed the eastern United States and really did get abroad. The while he lived gloriously and, withal, religiously. He impressed one as a sort of gay, young, and gallant monk without an order. Or perhaps his order was life and the world his monastery. I suppose he deserved little credit for his courage, his disdain of money and comfort, his laughter, for all these qualities were as spontaneous in him as smugness and caution are in you or me. Yet his life was his vocation. He created, wherever he went, a sense of the adventurousness and beauty of existence. He made people friendlier and drove not a few to generosity. And he inspired some young men I know to really noble ambitions. One or two of these ambitions will, I feel sure, be fulfilled.

I would have wagered with you that he would come back from England penniless and much wiser, that he would begin to see the folly of his haphazard life, that he would find himself some reputable office work and settle down to the normal, sensible existence of a good American citizen.

I was, accordingly, astonished when I discovered him on Park Avenue lolling in the tonneau of an unnamable foreign automobile, with a chauffeur and footman stiff-backed before him.

The automobile was a magnificent creation, very much like a Hispano-Suiza cabriolet, in ebony with the most delicate of white enamel and silver trimmings. The chauffeur and footman matched, even to the silver, the decorative scheme of the car. Blue lay deep in gorgeous pillows that were massed against the dark upholstery. He looked for all the world like a child in its first fine robes in its first fine baby carriage. His eyes were bright. I could see from his lips he was singing, singing perhaps some flamboyant song of his own making.

The car had rolled by when Blue caught sight of me. I was too astounded even to salute him. The car came up to the curb. Blue slid out to the sidewalk, kicking three blue-and-orange cushions to the street. They lay there, huge swollen flowers in the dirt. He looked like a college boy on a holiday.

"What do you think of it? It's my own idea," he broke out.

"What?"

"The automobile."

And this was his greeting after a year!

He had come over the road from Boston and hired, so far as I could gather, the entire Ambassador. Wouldn't I stop in for a bit to eat?

I stopped in for the bit, which was served with candles in his own private rooms. He had a whole corps of waiters for the two of us and a major-domo to run the show.

"Well," he was laughing at me from a lounge in the drawing room afterward, "what's your guess?"

"Crazy."

His eyes twinkled, "No. Not that."

"I give up."

"Behold a plutocrat. An uncle who made a fortune in Romanian oil left me five million dollars."

Sure enough. Blue had become a millionaire, although I found out afterward that his fortune was two million and was left him by a cousin. He had made it in Australia, where a great deal of it was in real estate and sheep holdings. Blue promptly turned every possible investment into cash, which he kept on check in numerous banks. He had a little library case of these checkbooks and was very proud of them. "I have more checking accounts than anyone alive" was his happy boast.

I believe he did. One day I counted sixty-three of these books on sixty-three different banks. It is remarkable what a man can do with money.

Believe me, Blue did some amazing things with his money. He bought three or four palatial houses and filled them full of run-down servants. He used only one of the houses, but he always saw to it that the servants had a good time. He bought his favorite mansion from an old Boston aristocrat, bought it with all the furnishings. It was overstuffed when he took it, crammed full of lumpy, useless furniture and atrocious pictures. Blue remedied all this by doubling everything. That is, if a room had ten chairs, he ordered twenty put into it. If a room had six pictures and two tables, he saw to it that there were twelve pictures and four tables. He carried out the former owner's designs to an amazing absurdity.

The pleasure of being around where so much money was thrown away drew me to Blue's company. At first I remonstrated with him. For I had the old-fashioned idea that money is something you treasure or use to acquire more money. It had never occurred to me that money was a handy medium of exchange. Blue, with his usual intuitive wisdom, knew all this. He exchanged money for everything possible. He exchanged it with the poor for their delight. He exchanged it with the helpless for lighter hearts. I thought at one time he was setting a bad example for other plutocrats. But the fear was unfounded. Nobody imitated him.

I came upon him in his library, lying on the floor with his checkbooks and a heap of marked papers around him. He was evidently in great glee. "I have spent just nine hundred thousand dollars in eight months," he announced, leaning back, his arms as stiff braces behind him. He was exultant. (I found out afterward that he had spent somewhat more than a million.) "And believe it or not," he continued, "I have a million left."

He built a little factory for the manufacture of toy balloons. Colored toy balloons were one of his great passions. He designed various shapes and color schemes and had the balloons made accordingly. His favorites remained, however, the plain round balloons with the plain bright colors. He would go out into the hills with hundreds of these balloons and, lying on his back on some high crest, set them off. He made up little ditties to sing with the launching of the balloons. I never have seen and never expect to see a happier man than Blue on his back on the green grass watching with enrapt bright eyes a gorgeous orange balloon fade in the hazy skies. Sometimes when the wind was toward the gashouse, he would attach a small bill, perhaps of fifty or a hundred dollars, to the balloons. This was a ritual that gave him great delight. On other days he would paint, in contrasting colors, rhyming couplets on the balloons and send these too off into the skies.

I suppose Blue had a purpose in all this business. He struck me sometimes as being suspiciously naive. He had the boyishness of the true mystic. There were those who thought him crazy. Whether or not he had a purpose, he certainly succeeded in producing a very definite effect on me. I have always been extremely fond of money. There's no question about a man's best friend being his bankbook. And yet I must confess this madcap Blue put the stuff in a rather bad light and made one feel that making it was a ridiculous and nonsensical business. I suppose it is a bit foolish to spend the few years one has here accumulating any commodity. But, then, a man wants comfort and the things money can buy. I told Blue this once, and he laughed until I felt uneasy. "My dear boy," he said to me, ten years his senior, "my dear boy, it makes no difference what you want or what you do."

"What do you mean?" I queried.

"What I said." And he laughed again.

I was in New York for a few months. When I returned to Boston, I made a call. McCarthy, his favorite butler, came to the door in his shirtsleeves. I missed the usual ornate uniform. I knew something was up. McCarthy told me.

Blue had given away the last of his money, sold all his effects, paid off all his help, and disappeared.

I had a devil of a time finding him.

A month or so later—autumn it was—I was tramping across Boston Common when, lo, before me, bareheaded, hands in his pockets, kicking up the leaves, is my friend Blue.

I took a delicious pleasure in trailing him as he slouched along. He had on a suit of clothes that was either very cheap or very expensive, a hempen effect. I discovered later that the suit was made by Mr. Blue himself out of the substance of three burlap bags. It struck me as being an excellent idea. I followed him up Beacon Hill a block. He took a couple of turns and stopped before a house that might have been owned by one of the Adamses, one of those flat naive affairs with a white door and a shiny brass knocker. It turned out to be a former residence of the Episcopal dean of St. Paul's and was now run as a decent lodging house by a large German woman. Before Prohibition it enjoyed an honest reputation even among the ancients who, unimportant though they are, still hold on to this citadel of Boston's glory. But since Prohibition— well, since Prohibition there are few of us whose reputations have not suffered.

Blue turned the doorknob. I touched his arm. He looked casually around. He smiled, as if he had left me an hour before.

"This," he said, "is the only place in Boston for a man to live in."

I looked him over carefully. He was exceedingly thin and a bit haggard, though his eyes were as luminous as ever. I asked him about his lost grandeur, his money, his establishments. He looked at me with that childlike look of his, his eyes straight at you but out of focus by yards.

"Come up," he said.

I went up. His quarters were in the attic. The furnishings of the room consisted of one bed with straw sticking out of the mattress, one chair, and an oil stove that, I imagine, Blue used for cooking, though I could see no signs of food. Perhaps Blue didn't eat anymore. I was quite willing to believe anything.

He motioned me most gracefully to the single seat. No courtier in a palace was ever more considerate of his king than Blue of me. After a while he began to laugh again. He stood before me, six lean feet of him in his burlap bags, his arms folded, twinkling at me, grinning at me. And then:

"What's your guess this time?"

"Crazy again."

I said this but I didn't mean it. He had many of the marks of insanity but somehow he gave you the impression that we were all crazy and he alone was sane. He seemed to have such a simple purpose in his life and succeeded so well in being very noble and very happy that one hesitated to judge him. After all, there are few things—except, perhaps, accumulating money and real estate and a little glory—that mean as much as being very noble and very happy. After a substantial bank account I can think of nothing quite as important as happiness. One has to give him some credit.

He laughed at my guess. I mentioned again the fortune he had thrown away. He held up his palms prohibitively as if he didn't want the subject mentioned.

"Those millions were a trial set me by my Lady Poverty."

He bowed politely as if to stress the sincerity of his words. He changed the subject.

"Don't you love it here?"

I could not summon much enthusiasm. "It would be better wouldn't it if you could see the gardens or the statehouse or the river?"

He was a little hurt. "Look!" he pointed toward a small skylight. "Didn't you notice this?"

I hadn't particularly.

He pulled his bed over until it was directly under the skylight. He threw himself hastily on it.

"Watch," he cried. "Watch." He looked up through the skylight.

I looked. It was nothing much, a bright square of blue sky with strings of cloud slipping across it.

"Isn't that glorious? At night I lie here and watch the stars fill the frame. One of these nights the moon will be there for me. I can think so quietly with my eyes on my own piece of sky.

"I was saying to myself last night how I didn't have any property, but I did own a piece of sky. It's odd how the window makes you think you are all alone with its frame of stars."

I mentioned how Hans Christian Andersen used to sleep in an attic with the stars similarly above him.

"Andersen would have made a beautiful Catholic," he said.

I could not see the point, so I held my peace. He began to talk, talk intensely, brilliantly, talk not as if he were talking to me but to some vast audience that hung on every word. He talked of life, the adventure of life, the loveliness of life. It is an old theme, but this lanky picturesque egotist touched it up with glory. The room grew dark in the dusk but his words lighted it. He filled the attic with his great courageous enthusiasm. What a small challenge death has for such a lad, I thought.

It was dark. He stopped suddenly. There was

quiet for a few minutes. Then a ripple of soft laughter.

"Was I preaching?"

I did not answer. I waited a minute and then said:

"Yes, life is beautiful. What are you doing to pay for it?"

I could hardly see him in the dark. Then after a while his voice came, and I had never heard it so grave, so, almost, tragic.

"Please, please," it begged; "what can I do?"

I wanted to give him the old advice: go to his confessor. But any advice seemed so futile when given to Blue. Instead, I took my hat and slipped downstairs.

I felt he would like to be alone.

It was still dusk in the street. Some students in a theological school nearby were practicing hymns. Lights were spurting out, street lights, window lights. I thought of the boy of the balloons and the limousines. It occurred to me suddenly that perhaps I was wrong about his self-sufficiency and that he needed someone. I turned and went back.

I knocked on the narrow door that led into the attic. There came no answer. I slipped in. The room was black except where at the end, above a tall screen I had not noticed before, there was a faint uncertain yellow glow. I was mystified. I walked the length of the room and looked.

Behind the screen was a tall black cross mounted on a slight elevation. It was a brutal, bare cross. Before it, to one side, burned a candle. And on the floor, on his knees, his hands on the floor, his head almost on his hands, his hair barely out of reach of the smoky candle, knelt the erstwhile gay and gallant Blue. It was a striking picture, the black cross, the black figure, and the splotch of yellow candle.

I drew back into the darkness of the room and waited. Blue made no sign or stir.

I tiptoed downstairs again and went down to the side of the river. It was cool there, and clear, and immensely open.

# Chapter 2

I first met Blue under odd circumstances. John Stuart and I were having a glass of beer together not far from city hall. John was with the *Sun* in those days and the talk touched, as it inevitably did, on Frank Munsey. We were talking of great failures, not the glorious failures you find in the research laboratories of the Rockefeller Institute, or in the literature departments of universities, or in the planning rooms of organizations like the General Electric, not the fine failures who have dreamed dreams too immense for themselves—too immense often for any mortal—and missed, but the failures who are thrust into greatness by the gods and are too weak to make any use of their fortune or too stupid to know what it is all about.

Munsey always represented an uninspired failure to me. It was as if someone had tried to pour a lake into a water bucket. Stuart suggested that the size of the bucket made, in an absolute view of things, no difference so long as the bucket was full. It is a way the scholastics have of explaining the varying degrees of happiness in heaven. John is a scholastic, and a brilliant one to boot. I was going to remark that New York wasn't heaven, not quite at any rate, when a voice at my side by the bar piped up: "I know a gent who's so happy he's almost crazy."

Happiness wasn't the burden of the conversation, but in those days no one was interested in carrying the burden of a conversation. Our new comrade, a sturdy little man with coarse ruddy cheeks and bright black eyes, looked up at us over one of Al's excellent free ham-on-rye sandwiches. His name was Stevens, as I remember it. He was, it turned out in talk, the superintendent of the Tootsall Building, a new thirty-story structure on lower Broadway. It was he who first introduced me to Blue.

One day (so Stevens told us by the bar), a tall lad with dark intense eyes and an easy nonchalant smile came to his office to rent some space on the roof of the building. He wanted to live on the roof. He had a tent he could pitch there, he said.

Stevens was baffled. No one was renting space on skyscraper roofs in those days, not for pitching tents at any rate. He thought him mad. But the lad insisted he was sensible and in earnest. He set forth the advantages of living on the top of a skyscraper: the air, the view, the solitude, the closeness to the heavens. He spoke vividly of his plans: how he could dream there on his back, how he would use the tent only on stormy nights, how delightful the music of the city would be, compressed by distance into a single note, how he could fly kites there and liberate balloons and set off Roman candles, how he could shout there to his heart's content and, even, pray there.

"The first thing I knew," grinned Stevens, "I was beginning to think of living on the roof myself. The boy with his spellbinding almost had me sold. But I remembered the wind from the Atlantic is a gale up there more often than not, and I thought of the fog that hangs on the tops, and I knew all elevators stopped at nine p.m., so I argued myself out of the coma. Think of climbing up thirty stories to bed!"

But the lad would not be dissuaded. Stevens had no way of setting a price on the location. He gathered that his visitor was anything but wealthy. Finally, he agreed to let him have freedom of the roof provided that he, in turn, would fill in on the elevators and polish brass when special polishing was needed.

"You'd think I'd handed him over the British Isles," said Stevens, "the way his eyes shone. 'How can I ever thank you?' he asked me. I told him to keep below the parapet up there or the wind would blow him into Ohio. 'That would be an odd journey,' he mumbled seriously. I looked at him sharply. 'None of this suicide stuff, now,' I warned. He laughed at me. 'Suicide? I should say not! I'm just beginning to live.'"

So Blue became a tenant of the roof of the Tootsall, thirty-story skyscraper, Broadway, New York City, New York.

He was a rare tenant, according to Stevens. He gave up the tent for an enormous packing case that he found somewhere in the building. Blue could stand up in the case and walk around in it with ease. He painted it on the outside a half dozen different colors but not without some pretense at design. It seemed to be covered with figures, figures of gaily garbed soldiers marching, all marching. The colors were brilliant and the effect arresting. The case looked like a glorified circus wagon. On top of it Blue had nailed a long broom handle as a flagstaff. From the flagstaff flew a white crudely cut pennon with the bold word *Courage* painted in red. It flew there, day and night, high over most of New York.

"There are higher buildings than ours," Blue used to say to Stevens, "but we have it on them. Our building is a fort." To Blue, that building rising up into the skies above Manhattan, towering at the time over all but eight or ten other structures, with its painted box and pennon on the roof and its red word *Courage*, was a citadel standing for something or other. It stood, I suppose, for what Blue stood for. It did not discourage Blue to tell him that to the millions of human microcosms that crawled up and down at the foot of his skyscraper the building was a tall structure and nothing more. "Anything so glorious as this," he said one afternoon out on the roof, "anything pushing up so into the stars and skies, anything subduing the sea and rivers and landscape as this does, must have a glorious significance." He waved a long arm toward the blue-black ocean creeping up New York Harbor, creeping up the East River and the Hudson River, he waved to the stretches of Long Island, to the cliffs of New Jersey, to the stone thickets of Manhattan thinning out westward into the hills and levels of New York State, spreading out westward over the world. "Must," he said, "must have a glorious significance."

Blue had a regulation hospital cot on which he slept. He pitched his cot in the southwest corner of the rooftop, close to the parapet facing the harbor. He slept in his packing case only on rainy nights. It was spring when he moved up, so the weather was with him.

I was interested in Stevens's tale, as you may imagine. Stuart was a bit bored. He had seen too many eccentrics in his day. After the incident of the band, John folded his newspapers under his arm and left to catch a train for Douglaston. But the incident made me more interested than before. I could catch glimpses of a curious wisdom in this lad Blue. I stayed.

Blue, according to Stevens, was very fond of band music. He would follow a vigorous band the whole length of a parade, never tiring of the blaring of the brass, the thumping of the drums. He especially liked martial music. His idea of one of the greatest offerings of life was a rich, full band with plenty of brass and drum and plenty of supplementary fifes, marching in gorgeous uniform, marching with high military bearing, marching down a broad avenue or boulevard out of the distance, metal flashing, uniforms flashing, marching proudly, nobly, radiantly, and playing some magnificent bizarre fighting tune. "The thump of it, and the pound of it, and the ring of it, and the call and challenge and command of it start my blood racing, start my feet lifting, start my eyes searching, my heart stirring.... Surely no man can deny there are things worth fighting for, worth dying for, who hears militant music like this." So Blue said to me in a lyric moment in later years when I knew him. I think it was the spectacle of marching uniformed men quite as much as the sound of marching music that thrilled him. Blue had little interest in form but he was ever hungry for color. A beautiful pool or splash of color, formless, accidental, would hold him enthralled. A chart of the spectrum, a red tile roof against a blue sky, an orange chalk disk on a school blackboard, a yellow hat under green trees, a spread of paint samples, weather flags, railroad signal lights, any sudden display of color would fascinate him, sometimes hold him as intensely as a sunset pageant or the shifting canvases of the sea. The spectacle of a colorfully uniformed band with dazzling brass coming down through the great shafts of sunlight and shadow of a high-walled avenue would lift Blue to another level. And when the music burst out, when it came tumbling like a gorgeous cataract down the street, Blue was happier than it is given most men to be on earth.

One day Blue invited Stevens to a little party he was giving on the roof. The time set was eight o'clock. Stevens stayed in town that night so he could attend. Blue had told him it was to be a private and exclusive affair.

Stevens arrived a little after eight. It was a hazy night, dark toward the harbor, dusky toward the sunset. Blue met him at the door on the roof. He was all courtesy and graciousness. His duties as host rested gaily upon him. He led him to a bench, borrowed from an office for the occasion, set against the parapet facing downtown. The light, such of it as came from the raised elevator shafts, was bad, and Stevens was almost seated before he observed a fellow guest: Abraham Morgenthau. Abe ran the newsstand at the subway entrance on the corner. He was a fat, undersized, talkative, good-hearted Jew of about thirty-five who was everlastingly puzzled and amused at Blue. They were devoted friends. When Abe's little boy Morris was in the hospital after his fall from the fire escape, Blue used to sit with him all afternoon telling him stories. Morris didn't understand Blue or his stories any more than his father did, but he liked Blue. Abe had no use for the tops of skyscrapers. It was only his affection that brought him there that night.

Abe and Stevens waited. They were the only guests. Blue was enthusiastic, rubbing his hands, talking. "This is going to be a great surprise," he explained to them.

"It was," said Stevens. "He disappeared through the door for about five minutes. When he came back he was arm in arm with one of the funniest things I ever saw in my life—a tall, cadaverous Negro, three or four inches taller than himself, and Blue must have been six feet—dressed in all the shiny braid and buttons in Harlem. There wasn't much light, but what there was sparkled on that fellow, magnified, as the pictures say, a million times. Abe was scared, I think. He moved around nervously. The tall Negro had a cornet slung by gilt cords across his epauletted shoulder and brocaded breast. Blue brought him over proudly. 'Friends,' he says, 'I want you to meet a great friend of mine, General Grant.' Then he introduced us. He wasn't fooling, not Blue. He was fond of this fellow. They both were all smiles.

"General Grant drew back to the center of the roof. He pulled himself up as high as he could, and believe me, it was some high. A strip of light from one of the shafts fell on him like a stage light. He lifted his cornet, tilted his head back, and began to play...." Stevens looked up at me with an intense seriousness. "I tell you I never heard anything like it in my life. Abe and I weren't laughing. I don't know what he played but it got me. And he could play it, standing up there, swaying.... The music was so startling, the whole thing so different, that I figured there must be a law against it and we'd all be pinched. You should have heard that music from that tall Negro alone up there. Abe was shivering. I felt funny...."

I can't duplicate Stevens's description. There wasn't much poetry in Stevens, but he knew when anything moved him. And I can imagine how that lone cornetist on the top of a skyscraper at night sending his music vibrating up into space, up into the stars, moved him.

Blue withdrew into the shadows until the general had finished. Then he rushed out. "Glorious! Magnificent!" he was crying. He shook the general's hand. "I'm proud of you," he said.

And then came the high point of the evening. The door opened cautiously. Suddenly, there piled out of it a dozen Negroes of all sizes and shapes, all dressed like General Grant, all with instruments, trombones, cornets, drums, cymbals, and all grinning. Blue stepped out to meet them.

"Abe was groaning," said Stevens, "and I was afraid Blue was going to jump off the roof or pull something more nutty."

Blue, it appears, had picked up a few dollars somewhere and had confided his idea for a "top-of-the-world band concert" (as he called it) to his friend Grant. Grant played in a band that suited Blue's plans. The result was the concert.

According to Stevens, there never was such a concert. The Negroes were able bandsmen. Blue, they knew, was a friend of the general. And the night, the height, the stars, the twinkling dark in the distance, the yellow haze over uptown Broadway, the silence made them outdo themselves. "The music blazed so," said Stevens, "that you could almost see it." Blue wanted wild militant music only—"maniacal music" Stevens called it—and he got it. It must have been overwhelming up there. I suppose none of the drab citizens who tramp lower Broadway at that time of night heard or suspected the magnificent tumult on the roof of the Tootsall Building.

It was a strange concert.

I was eager to find out more about Blue. Stevens, I said to myself, has some sort of vagrant on his roof, but he probably exaggerates his eccentricities for the sake of a good story.

"I gather from your tale that this fellow is crazy," I remarked, "but I don't believe he's the marvelous youth you make him out to be."

Stevens took up the challenge.

"Come on," he said.

We left Al's together. Stevens stopped for a minute to call up his wife in Flushing to tell her he would be late. There was a wrangle over the telephone. Everybody in the cigar shop could hear it. Everybody enjoyed it. Stevens came out of the booth unruffled. It must have been a daily ritual with him.

We reached the Tootsall Building in a few minutes. An elevator shot us up the shaft to the roof. We looked around for Blue. It was dusk. Finally Stevens spied him lying out on his back, on top of his packing case, his hands clasped under his head. I could see dimly the gaudiness of the case and could make out the line of Blue's body on top with his white face tilted up.

He came down in a jump.

"This is great," he cried, taking Stevens by the hand. "I've been lonesome all evening."

Stevens introduced us. Blue was enthusiastic. "Don't you like it up here?" he asked, searching me in the dark with his shining eyes—eyes that were keener, I thought, than most people suspected.

I confessed I did. Stevens and he carried on a conversation together; that is, Blue did the talking with Stevens answering rhetorical questions now and then. Blue overflowed with ideas. He wanted the owner of the building to build cottages on the roof for the scrubwomen and janitors. He had a plan that involved flower and vegetable gardens and a small playground and whatnot. All that was needed, he declared, was twenty-four-hour elevator service, and he felt sure the owner would not object to that. "Why," exclaimed Blue, "look at the good he could do!"

Stevens grinned. He knew the owner better than Blue. "If he knew you were up here," he returned, "he'd kick you off tomorrow."

Blue was worried. "I didn't know that," he said.

So the time went by. The more I listened to Blue the more I liked him. I liked his looks, to begin with. Anybody would. But besides that there was a certain spectacular quality—one might call it a certain spectacular sanity—beneath all his ideas that was novel and stimulating to me. This boy, I said to myself, is no mere crack-brain, however improvident and impractical he may be.

After a while Stevens went down. I was left alone with Blue. He elaborated further to me his plan for letting the poor live on the top of skyscrapers. With the proper walls and protection, he maintained, they would be more comfortable than in their slums. "And then," he declared, "think of the beautiful lives they would live up on these clean heights. Think of the customs they would build up and the literature they would create. Can't you picture a group of laboring men gathered together out over some cornice after their day's work, gazing into the sunset and making the tales and legends of a new race of people? Can't you imagine the women putting up their fragrantly clean washing in the lofty winds of a May morning? Can't you see the new games the children would play, the new gaiety in their hearts? Poor people with these horizons! Poor people with the whole beautiful world beneath them! Poor people up here in the skies!"

I suppose there are a million practical difficulties, even admitting the consent of the owners. But Blue made me see the poor living up there with him so vividly that I almost believed it true. Blue always made me feel that he, whatever the difficulties, could make any of his dreams come true.

The minutes passed.... Night had smothered the city, and the city gave up its protest in uncountable millions of bubbles and gasps of light. Below was glittering Manhattan. The east was black. The opaque hilly horizon of the west was razor-edged against a last gleam of cold white light. Destroyers rode the unbridged Hudson; ferries and small craft flecked her with light. The East River lay her dark secretive self—coddling her treasure, Blackwell's Island—lay a cool, lamp-spotted, many-bridged stream between the sprawling white conflagrations of Brooklyn and Manhattan. It was terrifyingly beautiful up on the roof, four hundred feet above the gaudy streets, four hundred feet up in the cool dark silences, four hundred feet up nearer the stars. What a freedom! One instinctively drew deeper breath. One instinctively expanded in stature, in gesture, in vision. The voice alone tended to grow small as if in reverence. There was little wind. The parapet was breast high. I leaned over it slightly to see Broadway below. I shuddered. Broadway was darker here. The great fountain of light at Times Square that inundated the uptown streets trickled away in these lower caverns.

Blue leaped up on the parapet, lightly with the aid of one hand. I shivered. He stood there smiling against the dark nothingness of the sky. He was talking, gesticulating. Then he laughed. He seemed twice as tall as before. "Behold," he said with a wave toward the harbor, turning as he waved, "the ocean, Italy, Spain, England, Europe. And now behold," he went on with another gesture, this time turning toward the west, "now behold the farmlands and the deserts, California, the Pacific, Japan, China, the Orient....

"What a view one has from here!"

Three or four stars popped out. One large one shone above the boy's head. He was superb.

"God is more intimate here," he addressed me from the parapet. "Don't you find him so? This is height without desolation, isolation without emptiness. I ride into infinitude on the top of Manhattan Island!"

He leaped down. "I'm so happy that you're here. I wanted to share my world with someone. It helps me to realize what a beautiful world I have."

He stood before me for a moment, watching me. Then he asked: "Are you a Christian?" I nodded. He said: "You're lucky. We're both lucky."

He put his hands into his trouser pockets and leaned backward, his face toward the heavens, now filling with stars.

"I think," he whispered half to himself, "my heart would break with all this immensity if I did not know that God himself once stood beneath it, a young man, as small as I."

Then he turned to me slowly.

"Did it ever occur to you that it was Christ who humanized infinitude, so to speak? When God became man he made you and me and the rest of us pretty important people. He not only redeemed us, he saved us from the terrible burden of infinity."

Blue rather caught me off my guard. I might have admitted in him a light turn for philosophy. I did not expect any such high-sounding speculation as this. But he was passionately serious. His eyes were glowing in the dark. He threw his hands up toward the stars: "My hands, my feet, my poor little brain, my eyes, my ears, all matter more than the whole sweep of these constellations!" he burst out. "God himself, the God to whom this whole universe-specked display is as nothing, God himself had hands like mine and feet like mine, and eyes, and brain, and ears!..." He looked at me intently. "Without Christ we would be little more than bacteria breeding on a pebble in space or glints of ideas in a whirling void of abstractions. Because of him, I can stand here out under this cold immensity and know that my infinitesimal pulse-beats and acts and thoughts are of more importance than this whole show of a universe. Only for him, I would be crushed beneath the weight of all these worlds. Only for him, I would tumble dazed into the gaping chasms of space and time. Only for him, I would be confounded before the awful fertility and intricacy of all life. Only for him, I would be the merest of animalcules crawling on the merest of motes in a frigid infinity." He turned away from me, turned toward the spread of night behind the parapet. "But behold," he said, his voice rising with exultancy, "behold! God wept and laughed and dined and wined and suffered and died even as you and I. Blah for the immensity of space! Blah for those who would have me a microcosm in the meaningless tangle of an endless evolution! I'm no microcosm. I, too, am a Son of God!"

He finished his outburst with a great gesture to the stars.

It was a full minute before he turned to me.

He must have seen the amazement on my face.

"I'm sorry," he said. "It's a sort of declaration of independence I make up in these high places."

I told him it was curiously impressive. He smiled. "I'm afraid it was rather long. Five years from now I shall probably be able to say all that in two or three sentences. Ten years from now I shall probably be able to sum it up in a line." He looked at me for a moment. "And fifteen years from now I shall probably keep it all to myself."

He was amused by this last observation.

"Imagine," he declared, "imagine anyone with anything good to tell keeping it to himself."

My head was in a whirl.

He had raised me to the clouds with his brilliant apostrophe. He had seemed like some lean dark-haired archangel. Then suddenly he was laughing....

Blue, I must confess, was too much for me. His exuberance and courage were overwhelming. Besides, the night was too beautiful, too beautiful up there in the freedom of heaven. The stars, the sky, the wind, the water and land strewn with their own stars, all had a freshness unknown to me before. I suppose it was Blue who with his magic gave them that. I had had too much for one night....

I left him with his big gaudy packing case and its pennon crying *Courage* to the stars.

The elevators were not running. I walked down the stairs. There must be a thousand steps from that high roof to the street. Yet I do not remember coming down. I remember reaching the street and feeling somehow that it was good to be down on the level of the world again. And I also remember bending back and looking up along the front of the towering building, looking up to where the distant top disappeared in the dark, expecting to see Blue.... It was madness, of course. But Blue made one believe almost anything was possible.

# Chapter 3

I left New York on business shortly after my first meeting with Blue. It was June before I saw him again.

He was on his knees on the roof painting a giant box kite he had made. He painted with energetic delight. The roof was splashed and daubed with the bright green paint. He was splashed and daubed with it. I had to keep several strides from him or I would have been similarly splashed and daubed. His face was streaked with green and his smile never looked merrier than it did through the paint.

"I am Spring," he laughed, "and I'm just starting out to paint the world!"

It wasn't hard to picture Blue tipping sky-high

vats of green paint down the hills and over the plains of the world. And how he would drench the world!

It was a brilliant afternoon with the roof like a float in the vast blue heaven. There was a gusty light wind chasing a half dozen white clouds northward high overhead. Blue finished off the painting of his kite with a series of extravagant brushstrokes that sprayed paint over the roof. He chuckled to himself as he did it. He was having glorious fun. And this, I said to myself, this is the passionately religious lad, the tall dark prophet who stood against the stars one night weeks before.... I did not know Blue so well then.

Blue announced his intention of flying the kite. That was one temptation he could never resist, he explained—the immediate flying of a new kite. "Who knows what a new kite will do? It may show powers undreamed of, special powers given it by accidental twists, fourth-dimensional twists, with which it may pull the earth off its orbit, lug it into the way of the sun and planets, set them crossing, colliding, crashing, blasting the whole universe to pieces. That would be a kite!..." While he talked he fastened the kite by a slender strong cord that he unrolled from a great wooden spool. "What a kite! The least this green dragon can do is to pull me off the roof, pull me up over the city, up over the Great Lakes...up over Canada...up over Alaska...up over the North Pole!"

He was still chuckling, delighted with his fancies.

Meanwhile he made the kite ready. He set it on top of his multicolored packing case. Then, giving himself plenty of free cord, he sprinted to the edge of the roof. I thought he would go over the parapet. But just as he reached the edge, the kite caught the wind and up it went in little spurts. The spool unwound madly as Blue fed the kite more freedom. He was still against the parapet. There came a lull in the kite's progress. Blue kept pulling in the cord and releasing it, pulling it in and releasing it to force the kite upward. Suddenly, cramped for arm room, he jumped up to the top of the parapet. And there, leaning backward over the city, leaning with nothing holding him but the uncertain pull of the kite on a piece of string, with four hundred feet of frightful space beneath him, he began to sing!...

I couldn't stand it. The sight of him made me dizzy. I sat down on the roof to consolidate myself, to convince myself that I, at least, was safe. I did not look up until I heard his footsteps behind me.

"You came mighty near getting your wish for

travel," I mumbled.

He did not hear me. His eyes were on the kite, now little more than a speck over the city. His face was serious. "I made a mistake," he said slowly. He looped the cord twice around a pipe on the roof and, sitting down, settled himself against the side of the packing case. "Yes, I made a mistake. I should have painted that kite red or yellow. It would look much better against the blue sky."

It didn't make any difference to me what color the kite was or, for that matter, what color any kite was. Besides, it was almost invisible. I said so.

"I know," he returned, "but think of all the people uptown who are looking at it. Think of them."

I could see no reason to think of the people uptown. I doubted, in addition, if anyone up there could see it either. But the afternoon was too beautiful for argument. I settled myself down alongside of Blue and relaxed.

He toyed with the kite string and whistled. Blue could not whistle. He could no more carry a tune than a bullfrog. He simply blew a shrill sound from pursed lips, sometimes loudly, very loudly, sometimes softly. His low notes on the intake of his breath were plaintive. His high notes were piercing. He would start bravely out on one tune, shift unconsciously to another, and end up in confusion. He knew I was following his efforts. After a while he turned to me. "I have no interest in time or key," he said. "Tones are what I like."

He was serious. I had to laugh: he sounded so much like a child saying, "Peppermints are what I like," or "Balloons are what I like." I have since noticed that people with an unusually strong love of color have most often little ear for music. Any taste they may possess is for obviously emotional, preferably sentimental, music. To them the world is visible music; to them, as to the poet, the stars are melodies and the sunset makes music in the sky. So it was, I believe, with Blue.

The sun wore down toward the horizon. Where the kite was I didn't know. I couldn't see it from my position. The cord seemed to be taut. Blue was in a garrulous mood. He was always loquacious, but usually he delivered himself more or less consistently on one general theme. But this afternoon, he hopped like a sparrow from one thing to another. I could not follow him. After a while I did not try.

He turned to me, for example, with: "Can you tell me what became of Saint Augustine's son?"

I told him I didn't know, didn't know, indeed, that Augustine had been married.

"He wasn't married but he had a son," said

Blue. "Do you know what became of Saint Francis Borgia's children?"

I had to confess ignorance.

"And what about Blessed Thomas More's family?"

Again I was at a loss. I advanced the information that some distant descendants of the English martyr had been devoted sons and daughters of the faith. That was all I knew. It seems that Blue had been reading about Saint Louis and his eleven children somewhere, and that led him off into speculation concerning the various husbands and fathers who were great saints. "It's odd," he said, "that nowadays there's no special appeal to sainthood for the heads of families. The idea seems to be that after a man is married little else than an ordinary good Christian life is expected of him. In the ripe wisdom of noble husbandhood should lie, it seems to me, rare seeds of sanctity...."

"You mean," I said, "every husband is a sort of martyr." I couldn't resist the old joke: Blue was so serious.

But he didn't hear me. He was off in a characteristic appeal for a special society for husbands and fathers under the patronage of Saint Joseph. "Why," he exclaimed, "a knowledge of saints like Borgia or More or Louis—statesmen, soldiers, leaders—would be better than a thousand sermons! What giants those men were in the world as well as in religion!" Then he added with a smile: "And what families they had!"

He wanted me to promise to write a booklet for the purpose of organizing such a society. I did not commit myself.

A little later he had another idea: the publishing of a deluxe edition of the New Testament. (Blue was that uncommon person: a reader of the New Testament). The edition would be printed in large type on beautiful paper and be magnificently bound and illustrated. "I would try to make it as beautiful as an edition of the writings of a French decadent or an Italian dilettante. I might even try to make it a bit exclusive. Certainly I should have the first issue purchased by subscription only." His eyes were shining. "You know," he said, "I really believe that people then would read the New Testament. Indeed I wouldn't be surprised if they discovered Christ. I'll wager a cult would spring up here in New York and other cities for the imitation of Christ. I can see the papers announcing the 'birth of Christianity.'"

"That was the cause of Christian Science," said Blue: "Mrs. Eddy happened to read the New Testament."

Then, without prelude of any sort, he asked

me if I didn't believe one meal a day enough for any man! "Note," he said, "how much clearer your mind is when you're hungry." Before I could even formulate an idea, he was arguing for the abolition of hats. Then he wanted to know if I ever felt peculiar before electric storms. And so, on and on. I cannot remember even a small part of the thousand things he talked about. Some of them were worth remembering. Some of them were not.

Most of his remarks were concerned with religious aspects of life. This struck me as strange in this age and generation. One expected that this striking and vigorous lad would have other diversions. He was audacious, merry, healthy. He had, indeed, all of those buoyant and vivid qualities I had been told were alien to religious recollection and the pious life. Perhaps my conception of the religious man was wrong. Perhaps he is the happiest man. I do not know. But I do know that it was Blue's philosophy that kept him from getting along in the world.

His obvious failure to become somebody, to attain a place in the community, was a source of constant regret to me. He would not practice even the most elementary economies that might have started him on his way to wealth. He would not, indeed, favor with special courtesy and thought those influential men who were in a position to help him. All he wanted was to be happy and to live out his philosophy as he saw it. Argument was useless.

He rarely listened to my exhortations and when he did it was with a quizzical face as if he did not understand my attitude. Yet my attitude was in no way mysterious: it was the attitude of everybody everywhere. Blue, I'm afraid, was not marked out for success.

Dusk came as we sat there that afternoon, came with a light fog out of the east. The kite had disappeared. The cord lay slack across the parapet. Blue was not the least interested. He was telling me a story. He had been talking about art and artists. He had little use for the art that is kept in galleries and museums and the halls of the rich. He had little use for that kind of art, he said, even when it was put up in a public square. The art he liked was dynamic art, the art that changed skylines, the art that created beautiful customs, that inspired men and women to love one another, the art, in brief, that transformed lives. The art that would do that tomorrow, he maintained, was the art of the motion picture. "Once," he said, "the cathedral builders and the troubadours, interpreting truth, created a beauty that was as current as language and almost as essential as blood. Then came the printed word to spread confusion, to throw a twilight over the world in which men became little more than shadows chasing shadows. But now we have a new art, luminous, vivid, simple, stirring, persuasive, direct, universal, illimitable— the animated picture. It can create a new people, gracious and graceful, sensitive, kindly, religious, a people discovering in beauty the happiest revelation of God. No art has ever had the future the motion picture has. If it fails, no art shall have had as great and lamentable a failure."

I did not subscribe to all Blue's enthusiasm for the motion picture. I knew, whatever he said about art, his weakness for pictures: he took more delight in children's picture books than any child. I chided him on his positiveness. He simply shrugged his shoulders. Then he told me this story.

It was a story for a motion picture, he explained. I shall reproduce it as best I can. I do not hope to catch the magnificence of it as he told it, there up on the roof with the fog settling aimlessly over us like a thin white smoke in the increasing dusk. I shall never, I know, have a story told me as vividly again.

The last known Christian had been put to death. (So Blue began.) He had been found living in a lower level of an abandoned mine in South Africa. He was ferreted out and brought to trial. He had professed Christ. There was no tumult or clamor. He had been locked in a lethal chamber. The gas was admitted. In a few minutes he was dead. He was found lying forward on his face where he had fallen from his knees.

The International Government of the World announced the capture and execution. "The work of a thousand years is now at an end," it declared in its exultant bulletin. The day of the announcement was a day of great rejoicing all over the earth. The IGW—as the International Government of the World was known—declared a half holiday for all workers. Great effigies of Christ on the Cross were burned at all the subcapitals of the world. While the crosses flamed, the multitudes paraded and sang. It was the first time in a century that singing had been allowed. The work of extermination was over.

It was a strange world that witnessed this day of jubilation. The peoples of the whole earth had become slaves of a few masters. They had been herded into vast industrial centers, great mountains of stone and steel, banding the round earth like mountain chains, rising like huge wens on the face of the globe. But these men and women were not ordinary slaves. They were creatures of the machinery of a mechanical life, inferiors of the machines they operated, subsidiary attachments to the monsters of a new age. The fantasy of the philosopher had come true: machines had become superior to men. Men were not mere automatons; they were minor automatons, servants of a mechanical state.

The masters of the IGW were the sons of the masters who had established the state. Their sires had done their work with brutal and consummate efficiency. All rebellious races had been exterminated. All people unsuited for slavery, primarily Latins and Celts, were segregated and slain. Only the stolid, unimaginative, automatic races, dominantly Nordic, were preserved.

The days of the ecstatic, passionate, beauty-loving, liberty-seeking peoples had, as was early predicted, come to a close. The sluggish, frigid races had survived.

The founders of the world state had prepared carefully for centuries. It was a long, difficult work to concentrate control of all fuel, food, arms, and transportation into the hands of six men. It was a chemist who, by a master stroke of strategy, finally perfected the consolidation. All agriculture and horticulture on earth were destroyed by a gas that obliterated a thousand square miles of forest in an hour. All fields, farmlands, gardens, and woodlands from the great wheat areas of Russia to the forest expanses of South America were turned into a fine powder that lay like mist along the earth for days and then disappeared. When the work was complete, the earth was as bare almost as it had been when the primeval glaciers withdrew their icy crust and first left the earth bare and bald beneath the sun. No fruit or flower or grain or vegetable showed itself. And none was allowed to show itself. The cultivation of any food growth was punishable by life imprisonment in the mines in the bowels of the earth. The cultivation of any decorative growth, flower or tree or vine, was punishable by death.

The few thousand inhabitants of the world who had not been corralled into the huge black industrial fortresses came across the dusty levels and valleys seeking admittance. They were counted, given numbers, and assigned residential vaults. At first, people stared at these sun-browned slaves from the fields. They ill-matched the white faces of the vault dwellers. But soon they lost their sunlight and became white as their fellows and as characterless as the numbers on their backs. No one had names. Individuals were known by numbers, and numbers only. There were no families. When children were born they were taken to be bred by the IGW in central vaults maintained for the purpose. If a child showed imagination or fire or spirit or brilliancy or any non-Nordic trait, he was destroyed. The multitudes, everybody except the masters and their large families and directing engineers, lived in steel chambers in enormous cabinets that were on the average a thousand feet high. These cabinets were like great filing cases. Each chamber was the same size as each other, was fitted with the same steel furniture, had the same bare walls. The chambers differed only in numbers.

No one wanted revolt. The lives the slaves lived were mechanical almost to unconsciousness. It was an existence that suited their racial type. But had some freak appeared, some heroic soul with a love of liberty, he would have been helpless. The master stroke of the chemist had made revolt unachievable. It was the perfect servile state: no one wanted revolt, and if anyone had wanted revolt it would have been impossible.

Perfect slavery was assured in this manner: the only food obtainable was liquid that was furnished through pipes, as was water, from a central reservoir. This liquid was of two kinds: a dark fluid that had lubricating qualities and a lighter fluid that had sustaining and fuelizing qualities. The formulae for these two fluids were guarded with a secrecy that precluded even an attempt at discovery. The chemist who evolved the formulae was killed immediately after final tests had proved their efficacy for the commonweal. (A huge statue was forthwith erected to his memory.) The king of kings, that is the master of Masters, alone knew the formulae. Anyone who made the least query regarding them was slain. The IGW forbade curiosity with the same rigor that it forbade laughter. There was little need for prohibition in either case.

When No. 862,337, say, arose at dawn, he went to a metal sink riveted to the wall. Over the sink were three pipes. One was water, one was the dark fluid, one was the light fluid. Before washing he took a glass of the dark fluid; after washing he took a glass of the light fluid. These two glasses were sufficient to provide him with sustenance until noon. At noon he took two more glasses. At night two more glasses. And so on, day and night, until he died. The slaves, I imagine, considered it a well-balanced diet.

The two fluids were very much like the oil and gasoline that were once used in automobiles. The airplanes that furnished the only transportation for the IGW used these two liquids for lubrication and fuel. When a driver left in the morning he took the same food he gave his engine. They both worked in pretty much the same way. Each industrial center was provided with a towering tank that served as a filling station. Each early morning would find a flock of airplanes buzzing around the top of the tank like flies over a dead fish.

If any section of the IGW empire ever became the least stubborn, not to say rebellious, these antiquated and Christian weaknesses could be quickly cured by shutting off the liquid food supply from the central reservoir. The slaves would immediately be without fuel or lubricant. It was a simple system.

Now it so happened, said Blue, after he had described the IGW to me, that like all mundane achievements the IGW had an imperfection. Even this kingdom of the Antichrist, perfect as it was, had a weak point. And so like all things mundane it came to an end.

The great capital of the IGW was SC No. 1, in what was once known as New York. Blue called it New York, and I shall. It is easier to say, for one thing, and for another, it (even such as it is) leaves a more Christian taste on the tongue. The weak point in the IGW was a small, thin-faced, wiry man who lived in a vault in New York. His number was 2,757,311. But Blue called him White for Christian reasons. White was one of the last of the sun-browned country dwellers to come in after all vegetative life on the earth had been destroyed. He had come with a strange group of people from one of the outermost places. The examiners at the gate had hesitated to let him enter. He had a light in his eyes and it was well known that no genuine IGW slaves had light in their eyes. They thought at first that he might have been a throwback to some destroyed race, but he had the proper credentials. They watched him carefully. In a few months he began to look like his fellow slaves. But the resemblance was only on the surface, said Blue, for his brain was afire and his heart bled.

White proved to be a good slave. He kept step. He walked with head bowed. He made no human noise that might soften the metallic din of the center. Winter came and went. White was beyond suspicion. But with the coming of spring he cast surreptitious glances sunward. At night he would look out of the ventilator at the stars. On Restday afternoon, he would go over to the hills across the western river. His fellow slaves could not understand his trips. "Why should he go over there," they would say to themselves, "when he could sit all day in the dark in his vault and stare at the floor?" But that was the extent of their inquiry. Thought was too much of an effort for them. Their sluggish minds would return with their eyes to the floor.

White had a purpose in the hills. He liked the open and the sunlight, though none of his fellows would believe it. But he had his eye out for something. One warm afternoon he found it in a distant valley miles from men: a small patch of brown moist earth. He knelt down reverently by it and made a sign of a cross on himself, touching his forehead and breast and shoulders with the first two fingers of his right hand. After a long while on his knees, he arose and made a sign of a cross in the air over the plot, murmuring as he did so. Then, with a glance at the airplanes that hummed by high overhead, he took a little sack quickly from his breast and sprinkled its contents over the moist earth.

"I shall bring God back to earth," White told the silences beyond the western river.

Then, he returned to Vault No. 2,757,311.

Spring grew into summer over the heaps of metal and flesh that were known as cities, over the bare rock and soil that was known as earth. The people in New York noticed that the air had become warmer, and that was all. Some of them scarcely noticed that. But White knew and noticed. And now and then he returned from his visits across the river with a light on his face that was increasingly hard to conceal.

Autumn came. The patch of moist brown earth was now white with wheat that rippled like water to the slightest wind. It was a small patch; no one had seen it on land, no one could see it from the air.

One Restday White visited his plot early. When he returned at dusk he carried with him a small package of thin white wafers. He had cut down his wheat and beaten some of it into flour; he had mixed the flour with water, rolled the paste into flat strips, and had baked them quickly over a fire made out of the remaining wheat.

White was jubilant that night.

He spent most of his sleeping hours on his knees. But the next day was a solemn day for him. It was the day on which the IGW announced the capture and execution of the last known Christian.

White spent the half holiday on his knees in his vault.

All afternoon he could see in the streets far below him the steady stream of black-garbed slaves, marching in slow step like prisoners, endlessly marching, monotoning their dismal paean of triumph. All afternoon the dark chant, varied only by silence or the endless shuffling of heavy feet, rose to his ears. And all afternoon he stayed on his knees. Now and then, he would look out and up to where above the black metal towers and roofs the sky still shone a lucent, unbesmirched blue.

Night came. White did not go to bed. He unpacked a box he had brought with him from the country. It held clothes, shoes, some tools. In the bottom of it, wrapped in an old coat, was a large case. He went over its contents carefully. There were some robes, a shiny cup, two small bottles, a book, a slab of stone, some miscellaneous small boxes and metal pieces. He went over each carefully. He filled one of the bottles with water. The other was already filled with a dark red liquid. Then he packed everything back carefully in the case and waited.

The city was as still as if death had stolen in and possessed it. White sat patiently through the night hours. The sky had a strange pallor, he thought, and there was a strange weight to the silence of the city. He did not know whether it forebode good or evil.

Two hours before dawn, he took up his case and made his way to the street. The streets were deserted. Always they were deserted at this hour as the slaves slept. But in the deserted dark of this night there was an unaccountable expectancy. The great masses of metal towered blackly upward, massed themselves hugely upward, as if threatening the stars. White walked quickly, a solitary speck of motion along the floors of the caverns of the monstrous city.

He reached the base of one giant structure that surpassed all others by a thousand feet, a memorial tower to one of the first masters of the IGW. He slipped into the only elevator and went hissing upward to the roof, a half mile above the earth. He locked the elevator at the roof so that it could not be summoned. Then he set himself quickly to work. He changed his garments. In a few minutes, despite the dim starlight, he was done.

"On top of that black tower of the devil in the kingdom of the Antichrist," said Blue, "after all those centuries of extermination, there stood a priest in amice and alb, maniple, chasuble, girdle and stole, heir in a noble line of Christ's servants, clad in their symbols of chastity, charity, honor, and faith. The figure of Christ's cross lay on his back. The anointment of Christ was on his soul. Before him was his altar, his case topped with altar stone and missal and chalice. On it lay the corporal with the wafer he had made from the wheat he had grown. By it stood the two cruets of water and wine. He waited until first there was a streak of light across the east. Then he bowed down before his altar. *In nomine Patris, et Filii, et Spiritus sancti. Amen.* The Mass had begun. He was keeping his promise to bring God back to earth."

Blue's voice was quivering. It was dark with night and fog. We still sat out on the roof. What time it was I did not know.

"The last Christian," said Blue fervidly, "was a priest. Can you see that heroic figure in the twilight of the world saying Mass in the citadel of the Antichrist? Can you hear the *Christe eleison* as he cries it to the breaking skies of dawn? Can you catch the murmur of the *Credo* as the winds carry it to the ends of the earth? Can you see him turning with shining face as he gives his *Dominus vobiscum* to the empty cathedral of the morning?

"It was magnificent," exclaimed Blue as if he were telling of something he saw. "And the while he is making the sign of the cross over the wafer of bread, the powers of the Antichrist are gathering. He has been seen.

"An early plane spied him as he bent over his altar in the first streaks of light. The warning has awakened the city.

"Below grows a tumult of multitudes. The clangor of the alarms and the rumble of moving people rise to the top of the tower. But the priest does not hear. His soul is on his Mass. The morbid slaves below awakening from their sluggish sleep are electrified by cries of 'a priest! a priest!'

"Millions who would not lift a hand to save a friend or give a sign of affection, these apathetic slaves of the Antichrist, are transformed by their discovery of the Mass. Stolid, stupid peoples, insensible even to pain, need—as ever—only the mention of the priest and the Mass to drive them into unimaginable fury.

"The mobs surge about the base of the tower. There is no access to the upper levels save by the lone elevator. Their blasphemies rise in raucous uproar. Their frenzy would hurl over the structure itself if it could…. The while the priest is reverently at his Mass.

"*Veni sanctificator omnipotens, aeterne Deus.* 'Come thou who makest holy, almighty and eternal God.' He is beseeching the blessing of the Holy Ghost.

"The Mass goes on.

"The Master of the IGW has summoned the marshal of his soldiers. 'Stop the Mass immediately!' he commands.

"The marshal reports that planes are speeding to the tower. 'The top is too small for a landing. It is a difficult shot...' he is explaining.

"The Master is furious. 'Bomb the tower. Destroy it. Demolish it. *But stop the Mass!*'

"His face was black," said Blue. "From his own tower he could see the silhouetted figure bending over his small altar. He tears his flesh in his rage.

"Two, three, four planes are circling above the tower. One drops a huge shell. It misses and goes hurtling down to the street. It crashes in the heart of the insane mob, annihilating a black square of them, shattering the steel walls, shaking the structures for a mile around. Another bomb falls. Another misses. And again, there are slaughter and destruction below....

"But now the priest bows low over his altar. *Qui pridie quam pateretur....* He begins the words of the consecration, the words that shall change the bread and wine of his altar into the body and blood of Jesus Christ.

"He approaches Christ's own words at the Last Supper.

"One plane is now low over the roof of the tower, so low that the crew can make out the figure of the cross on the priest's chasuble. A bomb is made ready....

"And now the priest comes to the words that shall bring Christ to earth again. His head almost touches his altar: *Hoc est enim corpus meum....*"

Blue was whispering. I think he was shivering.

"The bomb did not drop. No. No. There was a moment of awful silence. Then a burst of light beside which day itself is dusk. Then a trumpet peal, a single trumpet peal that shook the universe. Then the sun blew up like a bubble. The stars and planets vanished like sparks. The earth burst asunder.... And through this unspeakably luminous new day, through the vault of the sky ribbed with lightning came Christ as he had come after the Resurrection. It was the end of the world!"

Blue's last words were just barely audible.

"The kingdom of the Antichrist disappeared like ashes in a whirlwind. And hastening up out of their tombs and resting places came the souls of the just, happy, hearty, wholesome, to greet their king."

Blue paused. Then he added:

"Father White who had been No. 2,757,311 found himself a hero even in heaven."

So, he ended his story.

There must have been five minutes of silence. My body was cramped from its single position. My clothes were soggy from the fog. Yet, I had not noticed these things before. Blue was waiting for me to say something. I did not know what to say. I held my peace.

"Don't you think that would make a good picture?" he asked me finally.

He was close beside me, but I could hardly see him in the fog. I told him I couldn't tell. I suggested his theology was wrong. Isn't the church to endure to the end of time?

"But think of the possibilities! The scenes! The theme! Think of a picture of Christ and the end of the world!"

I had to be honest with him. I told him that it would make the sort of picture that would appeal to himself and the few others like him. Outside of that, I said, I doubted if it would have much success. "And anyway," I added, "don't worry. It is one of those pictures that will never be made."

We parted soon after that—I, to get some food and warmth on the street; Blue, so far as I could gather, to meditate further his strange dream of the end of the world.

His story was a great story as Blue told it. But I do not repeat it here because of that. I repeat it here because it gives a better insight into the mind of Blue than anything else I know.

# Chapter 4

On my next visit to the Tootsall Building Blue was gone.

I could not realize it at first. It seemed as if he must always be there like the roof and the sky above it. But Stevens had disappeared and the new superintendent refused to let Blue stay. He was afraid, he said, "that Blue might disturb the neighbors." I could picture poor Blue on the top of a thirty-story skyscraper in the business heart of New York disturbing the neighbors! At any rate, he was gone. Abe knew nothing about him. I could not find him.

I tried to find Stevens, too, then and since. I have always thought that he might furnish some valuable details of Blue's life in New York. But

Stevens had vanished. It seems that he was an inventor. One night he was trying to blow up the main vault of the Mansard Bank, which occupies the first two floors of the Tootsall Building, when he was discovered by the bank watchman. He told the watchman he had invented a new explosive—nitroglycerine, he called it—that he was going to give to Uncle Sam. He was only trying it out in the bank. The watchman was interested. Stevens told him to wait while he went for more of his explosive for a better demonstration. Nobody has seen Stevens since.

It was almost a year later before I saw Blue again. That was the day on Park Avenue when he drove up in his ebony limousine with silver trimmings…on his way, so to speak, to the bare black cross of his room on Beacon Hill.

# Chapter 5

There are people who say that no such person as Blue ever existed. There are others who admit his existence but maintain he was crazy. There is absolutely no question of Blue's existence. I knew him. I have no documents, birth certificates and the like, but I suppose I could find them. I have all his letters to me and his one serious poem, which he sent me without comment. The poem is signed "J. Blue," and I print it here.

### Verses
by J. Blue

*Human love is blind—*
*But how strange the love must be*

*Of the good and gracious God*
*Who died for the like of me.*
*So herein let us have hope*
*That our squalor find disguise*
*In the splendor of his heart,*
*In the glory of his eyes....*

Blue would have been tickled by the thought of anyone denying his existence. There was never anyone more alive than Blue. To those who maintain he was crazy, I have nothing to say. He was a stranger to almost all I hold sane and yet I have never known a saner man in all my life. If carrying out the first principles of religion and natural wisdom to their (for him) most perfect completion is insanity, as would be held by many an honest fool and dishonest liberal, then Blue was insane. But do you admit such a definition of insanity? Blue believed in humility and he was humble. He believed that nothing mattered outside of saving one's soul and making others noble and amiable, and he tried to do these things with more determination and uncomplaining courage than your captain of industry ever dreamed of, or ever could dream of. He made sacrifices that none of the world's heroes make.

Blue was not insane. His principles—and his

acts proceeded from his principles if ever a man's did—were as sound as the catechism. He was born a Catholic, but he had all that enthusiasm of discovery that heaven usually reserves for converts. His faith did not transform things: it made him see things. And what he saw made him exuberant with that enthusiasm so foolishly thought madness. Strange things happened to him. He invited them. His very character created them. This is not difficult to understand. Blue was glorious, and all sorts of glorious things attended him. His whole career is as obvious and reasonable as daylight—and as magnificent. I cannot explain further.

How he supported himself I do not know. Once, in a winter before he became rich, I found him shoveling snow. I know, also, that he did some backdoor begging. I suppose he thought this a penance of some sort, though I could never understand why. He was the happiest man in a kitchen you ever saw. He loved the homely smell of things. And the Swedes and Irish and colored folk of the well-stocked kitchens of Boston's Back Bay adored him. They would have given him their savings if he had asked. I can imagine these good souls and Blue: how beautifully they would get along together, how easily they would understand one another, how much laughter would be created

among them. They must have wondered sometimes
at their lanky visitor with his natural courtesy and
princely gestures, his laughing face and solemn,
strange eyes. They must have sensed, too, in some
subtle, vague way that Blue was no romantic vaga-
bond, though I doubt if they suspected that his
life was an amiable rebellion against all that their
masters and mistresses represented. He had taken,
I wager, his own vows of poverty, his own resolu-
tions for mortification. I cannot imagine to whom
he could have made a vow of obedience unless it
were to the Lord himself. Doubtless, his manner
of life without any obligation in obedience lost
him many graces. He might have joined an order
of some sort in time, though he seemed the man
to start a new order himself.

Blue, like most talkative people, disliked writing letters. He disliked writing of any sort. It has
been only after prolonged and somewhat unsatisfactory effort that I have been able to collect the
eleven letters of his that I now have. He wrote five
letters to me in all, one from England, four from
Boston and New York. The other six letters were
forwarded to me by some of Blue's acquaintances
who had read my advertisements and wished to
cooperate in this work. To these good men I now
acknowledge my indebtedness. No one of them

knew Blue very well, but each of them was eager to help in any way he could. It is not their fault that this tribute to Blue is as unsatisfactory as it is. I hope after the publication of this document that others will come forward, possibly even some who knew Blue in his early years, and volunteer their aid to a more fitting memorial.

I shall not quote all the letters at length. They are all rather brief and a few are almost entirely personal. It is interesting to note that Blue with all his naturalness of speech and gesture is formal and a little stiff in his writing. There are few of us who do not grow a trifle in importance when we take a pen in hand.

In one of his first letters to me Blue wrote a paragraph that reveals him more intimately than a dozen pages of my manuscript. He had been telling me how many of his best friends were derelicts, at the bottom of life. Then he writes:

> You cannot understand how hard it is for one to be practical who hopes for tenderness behind every face, how hard it is for one to be severe and profound who believes himself to be living a story that is glorious and true. Others can be impersonal, but not one who believes that he is on

an eminently personal adventure. Others can be important, but not one who is so small that he wonders why anyone save the infinitely kind God should be good to him. Others can be sensible, but not one who knows in his heart how few things really matter. Others can be sober and restrained, but not one who is mad with the loveliness of life and almost blind with its beauty. So others can live with wise men and important men, while I must always presume on those who are kind enough to forgive and weak enough to understand.

Later in this letter he says very beautifully:

Life gives you pretty much what you give it. She gives beauty to those who try to add to her beauty. She gives happiness to those who share their happiness with her. She gives, even, love to those who love her. But these are very, very few. Almost all of us have a capacity for being loved. But few of us have a capacity for loving.

It is in the same letter he writes of a mutual friend that he "had the old and admirable idea that a Christian should have Christian customs and manners, Christian poetry and pleasures, should live, indeed, in that fragrant and lovely flowering of the Christian life that is called Christian culture."

His second letter is extremely interesting—to me, at any rate. It is written on the stationery of the exclusive Hotel Ganymede. How he happened to be there he does not say. His handwriting is obviously excited. I had dropped him a note advising him to be more thrifty and urging him to take more thought for the future. He writes back:

> And even you preach caution to me! How I detest that word! How it has written its evil over our lives. Why, a man can't be spontaneously affectionate today without being suspected of weakness! We are advised to watch ourselves. We are counseled to keep our thoughts to ourselves. Silence, caution, reserve are urged as prime virtues. Our fear of exuberancy, of ecstasy, of any genuine passion is being stamped on our faces and our lives. We become a thin-lipped, close-eyed people. A thousand fine inheritances are being compressed into a single character—and what a thin weak

putty that character is! Once, I am told, men put on their shields and banners such brave words as *Love*, *Audacity*, *Faith*. Today we have written across a million pages and placards and billboards our slogans: *Self-considerateness*, *Thrift*, *Safety first*. We have about as much hunger for loveliness as a turtle. And about as much capacity for intense and varied living as a cabbage.

Blue could be positive enough when he felt like it. At the end of the same letter he adds a quieter paragraph on the same theme:

Conservative historians describe any man with a passion for greatness as a megalo-maniac. Conservative citizens regard such a man with suspicion. "Look at him," they say to one another, "the idiot! Why doesn't he settle down and establish himself in the community? Why is he forever restless, forever trying to get something beyond him? The man is crazy." These conservatives are partly right. Play life safe, and you'll keep out of harm. Be careful, be cautious, and you'll never die on Saint Helena. Your failure is measured by your

aspirations. Aspire not, and you cannot fail.
Columbus died in chains. Joan of Arc was
burned at the stake. Let us all live snugly—
and life will soon be little more than a
thick, gelatinous stream of comfortability
and ignorance.

His third letter is curious. It is nothing but a
scrap of wrapping paper with a half-dozen lines
scribbled across it. There is no salutation. At the
bottom just above the ragged edge is the one word
*Blue*. Blue's letters are on a strange assortment of
papers of all colors and sizes. His poem, for example, came to me printed out in blue pencil on the
back of a paper napkin. Here are the lines from
the wrapping paper:

> Men are terrified at suffering, at even the
> thought of suffering. Yet, through suffer-
> ing only can one attain wisdom. Through
> suffering only can one attain the greatest
> understanding. And without suffering it is
> hard to attain the kingdom of heaven.

His fourth letter was a reply to a note I had
written him in which I objected to his upbraiding
the world because it suspected all glorious gestures

and attitudes. The world, I said, believes most of its nonconformists are crazy and sometimes the world is right. He did not answer directly. He merely wrote:

> Most of us like to pose. And most of us when we pose are found out. And most of us, accordingly, suffer. Yet there is something to be said for posing. All poses reveal imagination. Some reveal vanity, to be sure, and some reveal humility. Every poseur does not deserve the black name of hypocrite. We meet a man who is playing at being hero or saint. The man may be tired of himself. He may know in his heart that he is not so good or great as he might be. His pose is an attempt at nobility. We laugh at him. But we are laughing at ourselves. It is because most of us are such poseurs to ourselves that we so readily find a poseur out.

His last letter to me is a letter from the Blue who wanted a moving picture of the end of the world. "And what after the end of the world?" he asks. The paragraph with his answer is, I am sure, well worth appearance in print.

When the day comes that the sky is emptied of stars, and the sun is black, and the distraught winds have only the void for their lament, I am sure that somewhere men will be merry together, somewhere good hearts will greet good hearts, and somewhere our dreams of unbroken love and good talk and laughter will have come true. This is a glorious Somewhere, and it is far nearer to us than the stars. There our Lady talks of children to unknown mothers who taught their many children the love of her single Son. There Saint Joseph is a man among peasants. There Xavier is home from his wars, and there Suarez and Aquinas have their arguments out. There Thomas More swaps jests with the older Teresa, while the younger Teresa gathers her roses. There Saint George boasts of his conquest of the dragon, and mayhap the Good Thief listens, or mayhap he hears little Saint Francis singing his songs. It is a good place, this Somewhere. It has been called Paradise. It has been called the Tavern at the End of the World. And it has been called Home. It is only Catholicism that would ever allow the like of me to hope some day to be there.

Blue must have had many friends. No man as generous of himself as he could have been long without them. Yet, he seems to have had few intimates. Friendship was one of life's fine things to him, and yet he did not look upon it altogether as the rest of us do. Sometimes, I think, he was a friend out of charity. Once, I gathered from his conversation, he had been mistaken in a friend. But he looked back on the treachery of the man he loved more with kindness than with pity, and more with pity than with grief. "Friendship, at worst," he once said to me, "is an investment. Your friend, no matter how he may turn out in the end, is an addition to your life. He brings some things, and whatever his disloyalty, these things he cannot take away."

Once I met Blue riding around with an unimportant little snob who had inherited some money. He was an immediate and constant irritation to me.

He seemed to think he deserved some credit for having the money he did not earn. He was offensively good-mannered—a trait common in men who have a passion for dancing attention on women and who, usually, cannot boast a genuine man friend in the world. He was using Blue, I surmised, as an exhibit. I mentioned this to Blue. He laughed.

"What a Christian you are!" he exclaimed. I think he was a friend to the fellow out of kindness. "I suppose you consider the exhortation 'love your neighbor' a figure of speech. You would love only the lovable. Did you ever try to love someone who was mean, petty, shallow, selfish? Try it."

I told him I was willing to try to love a villain but that I could not arouse any affection for a mere annoyance, an irremediable nobody. "I think I could love a lion," I said, "but I doubt very much if I ever could love a mosquito."

He regarded me seriously. "You consider yourself too much," he returned. "You could love a great enemy. Any healthy man could. Men have boasted that they were to be slain by Caesar. But one needs more than vanity to love a…a…what you call a mosquito."

He meant, I suppose, that I needed special graces in charity and fortitude. But the topic to me, being a poor Christian as Blue intimated, was distasteful. I let it drop.

Blue was, I happened to learn, particularly fond of two Jewish lads. He was forever extolling their virtues. "No one," he said to me once, "is more generous and more loyal than a loyal and generous Jew."

It is to these men that I am indebted for

three of the Blue letters. One, Mr. John Stone of Roxbury, Massachusetts, sent me this interesting passage from one of Blue's letters to him on the motion picture. Mr. Stone had, I gather, contemplated investing some money in the film industry. He mentioned this to Blue. The following long paragraph is the result. That Blue's remarks have no concern with the motion picture as an investment is typical of his impractical method of viewing things. Blue could see anything—even the motion picture—in terms of eternity!

> No printed word shall wring the new masses as did the printed words in the past. They have not time for the printed word. The day when a pamphlet distributed at a street corner could start a revolution or a new religion is over. The printed word is too common to be any longer compelling and too slow to be any longer dynamic. If you want to reach the masses you can reach them through pictures. These new children can be bent and molded as they sit in the dark enrapt before the magic of the mobile screen. There, in the dark, they can be lifted out of their daily servitude. There, they can be raised high above their

stone-and-steel environment. There, they can be brought to the high places and shown the deeps beyond the hard horizon. There, they can be taught to be superior to the great magnificent monsters that are their creations. There, they can be taught to love this terrible new civilization, because there they can be taught to look upon it as their child and not as their master. Here, then, is a mission for any agency. Here is a destiny for an art second to none in history. For it is given to the motion picture to save the soul of a civilization!

There was one thing Blue could not view with Christian forbearance. That was bigotry. Any manifestation of bigotry against any color or creed would send the blood to his face. Mr. Casril Wein, the second of his Jewish friends and also of Roxbury, Massachusetts, very kindly forwarded me this letter from Blue on bigotry. I quote one paragraph, which is enough to indicate the intensity of his feeling on the subject.

There are natural excellencies that exist without especial support from heaven: amiability, for example, and generosity.

And it seems that there are natural vices that beset man without any especial spiritual depravity or intervention of the devil: timidity, say, or querulousness. But as there are the supernatural virtues, so there are what one may call the supernatural vices. At least there are vices that cannot be traced to indigestion or anemia, or to misinformation or to ignorance. Meanness is one such vice; boredom, another. But at the head of the list is one of the most vicious of vices, and that is bigotry. The cruelty of that hatred of one's fellows that we label bigotry is so intense and so devastating that one, in quest of its cause, must pass beyond the ordinary depravity of the world and the flesh and look for that cause in the devil.

To Mr. Wein I am also indebted for this defense of loquaciousness by Blue. Blue was talkative. It is only natural that he should defend himself. Besides he had an antipathy to silent men. They were silent, he maintained, because they had nothing to say. Silence to him was a mask of vacuity. He was constantly amused at the success of the ruse. All the greatest men of the world, he maintained, were talkers.

It is the humble man who risks his dignity to speak up for what he loves. It is the courageous man who dares contradiction and the acrimony of argument to defend his beliefs. If one loves anything, truth, beauty, woman, life, one will speak out. Genuine love cannot endure silence. Genuine love breaks out into speech. And when it is great love, it breaks out into song. Talk helps to relieve us of the tiresome burden of ourselves. It helps some of us to find out what we think. It is essential for the happiest companionship. One of the minor pleasures of affection is in the voicing of it. If you love your friend, says the song, tell him so. Talk helps one to get rid of the surplus enthusiasm that often blurs our ideas. Talk, as the sage says, relieves the tension of grief by dividing it. Talk is one of man's privileges, and with a little care it may be one of his blessings. The successful conversationalist is not the epigram maker, for sustained brilliance is blinding. The successful conversationalist says unusual things in a usual way. The successful conversationalist is not the man who does not think stupid things, but the man who does not say the stupid things he thinks. Silence is essential to every happy conversation. But not too much silence. Too much silence may mean boredom or bewilderment. And it may mean scorn. For silence is an able weapon of pride.

There are two letters that are both rather heavy and rather long. Blue must have been in a pedantic mood—a rare mood for him—when he wrote them. One is sent in by Mr. Albert Considine of New York City. Mr. Considine first met Blue, he says, at a hockey match. Ice hockey was a game, Mr. Considine tells me, that had a tremendous attraction for Blue. The letter has, however, nothing to do with hockey. It has, among other things, a commentary on the neglect of laughter in history and is shrewd for a man who read as little as Blue.

People remember sorrow much longer than they remember laughter. It is easier to revive your sad hours than it is to revive your gay ones. It is too bad, with all the amiability in the world, that tears should be so facile and laughter require so much effort. Literature is to be blamed. It has never cooperated with the gayer side of mankind. The biographer is to be blamed as well as the poet and novelist. The biographer devotes his pages usually to the serious thoughts and undertakings of his subject. His laughter, however much or little it may be, is rarely re-created. The biographer exaggerates the serious side of man to give him importance, for it has always been felt, peculiarly enough, that seriousness is a sign of importance. The biographer stresses a man's work so much that the reader is led to believe that the subject did little else. And yet all men loaf far more than they work. All great men especially. It is a misfortune that the seriousness of men lives after them while their gaiety dies with them. There is great need of a new school of biographers. And there is, similarly, great need for a new school of historians. The history of the past, especially of the distant past, reads much like a long and somber obituary. And yet, those men of other days were as gay and gayer than we. As with individuals so with peoples: their gaiety dies with them but their seriousness goes on forever. Historians describe early peoples as especially severe, gray creatures moving stolidly through laughterless twilights. Yet, the presumption is that early peoples, especially the so-called primitive peoples, were immensely much happier and heartier than we. Primitive peoples as we find them in contemporary life are most always gay. The older a civilization, the more it approaches the glumness of stagnation. Capacity for laughter could well be employed as the index of the wisdom of a man or a civilization.

The other letter was written to Dr. Frederick W. O'Brien of Boston on Blue's returning to him a copy of Thoreau's *Walden*. It has to do with Thoreau, of whom Blue seems to have known quite a little. It commends Thoreau's meditation on the pages headed, "What I Lived For," and then goes on:

Now and then, a writer with an imagination on fire gives to truth a brilliant and spectacular beauty that is at once arresting and audacious. Such men are rare. And it is well to notice that it is their imaginations that are on fire, not their minds. For truth lends itself no more to theatricalism than the mountains, despite the psalm, lend themselves to dancing. Particularly grotesque Chinese lanterns seen across the lawn of a summer's night may appear arresting and audacious. But they are only Chinese lanterns. They decorate and beguile. They distract attention from the modest stars. But the stars are steadfast. They are mighty masses stabbing darkness with tiny dagger points. To the searcher for sensationalism, they may be monotonous. But they move the thoughtful man to profound speculation and they make him humble. Modern ideas, with all the flash and sudden attractiveness of novelty, are Chinese lanterns. Truths are like the stars.

We are indebted to Mrs. John Murphy of Ruggles Street, Roxbury, Massachusetts, for this last letter.[†]

Mrs. Murphy runs a lodging house for "men from the yard." These are, I understand, men who work for the railroad nearby. Recently when Mrs.

---

[†]  Anyone who possesses further information of Blue of any sort will do a great kindness to Blue's friends by communicating with me.    M. C.

Murphy was "doing" the lodger's room she came across a biographical note I had written on Blue. "I knew him in a jiffy." she says. "He was with me for a few months after the war. A brave smiling lad. I thought he had the consumption. He was the kind. But his health was of the best."

Such was her picture of him.

Blue puzzled Mrs. Murphy. She judged him one of those boys who always mean well but who, as she put it, never pay the rent. Mrs. Murphy is a trifle hard. Anyone might be after thirty years in a lodging house. She's a big round woman whose shrewd eyes belie the heartiness of herself.

"I spoke to him one day," she says, "how the rent was due. Oh, but he had a smiling way with him. It would melt the heart of a wheelbarrow. 'I forgot, Mrs. Murphy,' he says. 'I forgot. Honest. I asked my mother this morning for it.'

"Sure enough, he had the rent next day. He wanted to pay me double. 'Let's be good friends,' he says. 'It's black, bad business this money. Do you see how it comes between us?'"

Where Blue obtained the rent Mrs. Murphy never did discover.

"His mother had been dead twelve years or more, he told me once," explained Mrs. Murphy. "Perhaps his asking his mother was a joke of his.

He was always a-joking. Once big Jim Dineen, a fine strong good-living man, hit O'Brien and O'Brien drunk. Blue picked up O'Brien, picked him up the good-for-nothin' like you would a child. 'Poor Dineen,' he says to O'Brien, 'poor Dineen, but I feel sorry for him.' And the rest of us feeling sorry for O'Brien.

"A strange lad he was, indeed, a strange lad."

Blue left Mrs. Murphy's establishment abruptly. That is, he went out one day and no one heard from him thereafter. "His rent was paid up and beyond," says Mrs. Murphy. "And the things he left were of no use at all. I couldn't give them even to the Salvation Army much less to the Sisters. A shirt, a hair brush, and a pair of socks. He never had much, poor fellow, but he always looked well. Wholesome, I mean, and company-like. I think it was how we used to look at his face and not at the rest of him."

But one thing he left that Mrs. Murphy kept, bless her. That was a long letter, typewritten and addressed to "My good dear Mother." I can picture Blue walking in to a public stenographer with his manuscript and asking her to typewrite it. And I can picture the stenographer as she made the copy. Mrs. Murphy, had she a little more imagination, could have discovered in the letter who it was who paid Blue's rent.

I must confess I liked the letter. I find a quality in it that wins me. Blue, properly directed, could have made some money out of his talent. I think he could have run a successful column on a daily newspaper. He had the human touch, which could have been very fruitfully capitalized.

The letter goes:

> My good dear Mother,
>
> I have never liked any painting or statue of you I have ever seen. It is not that these representations disappoint me.
>
> That would be natural when I expect so much. It is that they touch me in no way at all as you have touched me yourself. I have no clear conception of you. Yet you are more real to me than the people around me. Oh, much more real than they. A thousand times, a thousand more real than they. Sometimes, it is true, my imagination supplies me with brief fancies of you. But they have no permanence. I do not keep them for my prayers. Yet even these brief fancies are unlike any representation of you I have ever seen. Sometimes I have a quick picture of you as a mother with your face lined and worn with sorrow and your hair gray. You are a little woman, bowed, but your

eyes are full and clear with understanding. I suppose the theologians would object to such a representation of you. Many little mothers like this have I seen and I cannot tell you how my heart has been hurt for them. They, too, have come back from their Calvary, poor creatures, neglected and mute, paying the price of great love. I know that you, Mother, regardless of the theologians, will understand this picture of mine of you. You know these mothers who love you so. You are the Mother of them all.

Then I have another glimpse of you. You are a young mother, robust, active, with smiling eyes. I think Hilary Pepler has this picture in his verses:

*Our Lady was a Milkmaid,*
*a peasant girl, and poor,*
*she whom Almighty God obeyed*
*would scrub the dairy floor.*

*Our Lady well could merrimake*
*and sing sweet songs to Him,*
*of butter, cheese, and curdle cake,*
*of how to milk and skim.*

I am sure you like Pepler's various verses

about you. I wish I could write as well as he can. There would, then, be no need of this letter. But this quick picture of you as a young mother, which I have now and then, is extremely vivid. The main quality of it is your activity. You do not sit drearily. You do not move sanctimoniously about. There is a certain health and almost exuberance to your actions. I expect you to come right up and speak to me.

You know John Mickel who has the candy shop on the corner. John claims he saw you one night. The people say that John is queer. Maybe. I know he used to limp a little before he met you and he doesn't limp now. I know, too, that you've come to many people. And it's always struck me as especially appropriate that your most important visits were to humble, common people. You might very well have come to John.

John, you know, doesn't talk much about it. The story is in his eyes though. Once, he told me how it was. He had been over to see his sister who was ill. On the way home, you came up to him. "Hello, John," you said. He felt absolutely natural with you. I can imagine that is the way you would come to people. You would call them by their first names. John is a good man. I think he's a saint. But you know more about that than I do. And if you really did visit John, you have a very good reason for it.

All of this is apart from the purpose of this letter. I simply am telling you that I have no definite picture of you as I write to you. But, Mother, you are so real that if you withdrew your support I think I would actually fall down on the floor here like a man in a faint. Dear Mother, how have you endured me all these years! Only for you, I would have long been lost. For you it is who took me and led me out of strange ways and darknesses years ago. You it is who takes me by the hand now day by day. Only you would not grow tired of the like of me—of anyone so sinful, ungrateful, selfish. I'm afraid, Mother, of your Son. I should be afraid of him. I would not dare to lift my head were it not for you. For it is you who stand between me and his terrible justice.

You see I cannot make myself clear to you. But I know you know I am not trying to be humble. The thought of my sins smites me down so that if there were not you I think I would fall into despair. And when I try to reason why you should continue to protect me I end in confusion. I can only throw myself on your love. I can only kneel and cry out: "I don't deserve anything. Not even the greeting of a stranger. But, Mother, without you what am I going to do?"

This is mad, isn't it? This is unreasonable. But I am helpless in my weakness. I, cowardly, feebly, selfishly, give the weight of my sins to you.

The other day, Mother, I was thinking of what people would say when I'm dead.

So, I thought I would leave them a line for my grave. That is, if I have a grave. I don't care one way or another. But I do wish someone would write these lines about me somewhere:

*Never was there a worse sinner,*
*And never was God kinder to one.*

Mother, it's true. You know how true it is. You are the only explanation of God's kindness to me.

So Blue's letter ends. It is typical of Blue— begins by accident and ends up in the air. But I think it makes good reading. You see what I mean about Blue having the human touch that could be capitalized. They say humor sells best nowadays.

But I really think that Blue's sincerity, under astute management, could have been made to pay dividends. You meet plenty of witty men but very few sincere ones. I am sure I have an idea here.

Mrs. Murphy does not agree with me. She knows men, she says, and if ever there was a useless one, it was Blue. She is still wondering how on earth he ever paid the rent.

Here, then, before me are these eleven letters, a motley queer eleven, the letters of an unusual lad. I knew Blue's faults as well as any man: his improvidence, his erraticism, his impracticability. I mourn that he did not put his mind to business. He might have left us a great legacy of commercial achievement, a noted name in the history of the practical progress of the world. Instead he has left us only these ragged letters, such as they are, and the memory of his strange self.

# Chapter 6

We were tramping out in the Newtons, out around the twin reservoirs that they call lakes. Dusk was sifting out of Boston and giving the massed trees—of which there are plenty in Newton—that stealth and secrecy that is their pretense at night. Boston College, with its solid Gothic tower, stood black against the last smoking flame of the November sunset. We were down in the dark. But no one could mind the dark, even of November, with the Gothic that dominated the hill. Blue caught his breath at the magnificent silhouette.

"That gives me courage," he said, with his face up toward the hill crest. "Of late I have been melancholy with autumn—a sign of adolescence or old age. But I couldn't be melancholy with that above me. Not that I care for the Gothic, but for what it represents. Sunsets may flare, and the blackness of hades eclipse the earth, but that will endure."

"An earthquake could toss it into the lakes," I objected.

"And so could the cataclysm at the end of the world. And so could a madman with dynamite. But where that stands there will always be something, though no stone is left upon a stone."

Blue is a mystic, and mystics while they appear crystal-clear are sometimes difficult to understand. He saw my shrugged shoulders.

"No great battle for a great cause can ever be forgotten. That up there is no mere group of college buildings; that up there is a battlefield, a sanctuary; that up there is a hearth and home for the Lost Cause that is never lost, the citadel of a strength that shall outlast the hill and rocks it stands upon.

"A great desolation grows about us but up there is the warmth of a fireside and the loveliness of a garden. There are shrines for the devout, but up there is a shrine for those who are going to war, for those who will see the shivering void beyond the rim of faith. Once heroes built fortresses against the Mongol and the Saracen; now they must build fortresses against the whole world. Once they fought with spear and pikestaff against hordes of riding men. Today they must fight against pride and indifference and knowledge, against the agnosticism that like a poison gas decomposes the minds of the earth.

"I tell you I know what I am talking about. Once they—the believers, the students, the scholars, the soldiers, the saints—could fight heresies and heretics. Today they have to fight a state of mind. One might as well fight a plague with a bow and arrow...."

Perhaps I did not get Blue's conversation correctly. I think, however, one can discover some of his meaning in what I try thus crudely to quote. I, who have fooled somewhat with the printed word, suggested books and magazines and newspapers as weapons.

There was the nearest thing to scorn in Blue's reply that I have ever heard from him.

"The printed word has ruined the intellect. It has given fools and fiends the same power as wise men and saints. It has made a jumble of the mind, a burlesque of reason. No one any longer knows how to think clearly and cogently to a finish.... Remember Christ wrote nothing except those mysterious words on the sand. One gesture of Saint Francis of Assisi is greater than a tome. Napoleon knew this. When he wanted to change the map and mind of Europe he did not begin by writing books. The astute man contemplates writing only when his useful days are over.

"You are interested in preaching and teaching. I'm not. An amiable good life does more than all the religious newspapers printed...."

"But you're preaching just now," I inserted. "But not teaching. I don't believe you. We have the printed word. Everybody employs it. We must. There is no way out except by rhetoric...."

He smiled. "I suppose I was preaching. I like to hear the sound of my voice—especially in a fragrant stillness like this. I really know little about the whole business. I suppose the truth is that the printed word was good for something once but it isn't any more."

He was laughing again. "If *you're* so interested in reformation," he went on, "why don't you start a school of religious art here in the United States? All heaven knows we need it. Hire a floor in the Woolworth Building or in the Bush Terminal Building, in some majestic structure built in the spirit of the age. Round up a dozen full-blooded huskies—lads with courage as well as sensitiveness. Share your vision with them until they are on fire with a Pentecostal ardor. Then, put them to work under a great banner: *We Ourselves.*

"I am speaking figuratively, of course. You can't make artists merely by lecturing at them. But something should be done. Youth is crying for fertilization.

"There must be young men today who are manfully and spiritedly religious—industrious, amiable, exuberant lads. Find them. Dynamize them! Tell them to be loyal sons of their age as well as their religion. How else can they be great in art?"

Blue was vigorous. He was intense—almost oratorical—in his speech.

"The poet saw Christ on the Thames. We might find him on the Hudson or the Charles. We might meet our Lady by the lakes here—as once did a boy at Guadalupe and a girl at Lourdes. The sight would be our reward for being loyal to our faith, our life and age. So, too, comes the vision to the artist!

"Tell your artists to immerse themselves in the fresh waters of the faith and come up vibrant, clean, alert to the world around them. Then they are ready to design or paint, to carve or write or compose, ready to interpret eternal truth in living terms, eternal beauty in vivid images of the present. Great men dominate their age with their own art. But their art, when great, is almost as much of their age as it is of themselves. They do not achieve greatness by fleeing the present or by bowing down in timid affection before the past. They do not try to cast their minds and imaginations into classic molds or Gothic molds or Renaissance molds. No. They take contemporary life avidly into their arms...and out of the union is born their art."

Blue made a gesture up toward the Gothic that dominated the hill.

"Gothic was an interpretation of the faith in medieval Europe. What architecture have we now that is an interpretation of the faith in the modern world? None. Saint Patrick's Cathedral is an anachronism on Fifth Avenue. The Cathedral of Saint John the Divine rises a huge and blundering anomaly. That they surpass the monstrosities of American ecclesiastical art does not justify them. They have a beauty, it is true, imitative and borrowed though it be, that towers above the broken spirit of church structures that are little more than compromises with Mammon. They *aspire*, at any rate. But why these ancient forms? Gothic is not an article of faith.

"Is this the vision that is to vivify contemporary American life? Has the final architectural expression of the religious spirit been made? Was the last stone in sublime church architecture laid seven hundred years ago? Have we no greatness to contribute? Has all steam and oil and electricity, all this building and expansion and industry, all this vision and invention and labor, all this creation and munificence, brought not one small thing to the house of God? I cannot believe it. (I speak only of church architecture. The other arts are beyond comment.) Something is wrong with your artists. It is cowardice to blame the age. Perhaps it is their art. Perhaps it is the dryness and dullness of their souls...."

On and on he went. We circled the lakes twice. I was hungry but I hated to interrupt. I disagreed entirely with him on Gothic. But I did not want to argue. Blue was usually wrong when he talked a great deal—and who isn't?—yet he always managed to say some things worth remembering. He gave me several ideas: that one about the artists, for example. Catholicism in the United States cannot be very deep or ardent or it would have flowered out into some sort of modern painting or architecture. And another idea he gave me is worth thinking over: the idea that it is growing harder and harder to keep the faith. As Blue said: "I tremble when I think of the boys a century from now." Scientific agnosticism is here for a long stay, he maintained, because it is not a philosophy but a somewhat vainglorious state of mind. It is hard to oppose it with reason and argument. The only thing to oppose it with—as he pointed out—is another state of mind. And that, I suppose, is where great lives and good art come in.

I have reproduced too much of the haphazard conversation of Blue, but I have done it with a purpose: to show that Blue, while he may not have sat long hours over books, was nevertheless somewhat of a thinker on his own account; not a profound thinker, to be sure, but keen and independent.

As to books, he once said: "Books are for people who cannot make up their minds or have no minds to make up." He regarded most reading as a form of parasitism.

We took a street car at Beacon Street and ended up in an old oyster house downtown. It was the oldest in Boston, I believe. The food was a very reasonable compromise between quality and price, and I enjoyed it. Blue did not eat much. He finished half a clam chowder, nibbled a few crackers, and passed up the rest. He was extremely serious, as he had been all evening. Such sustained seriousness was rare in Blue. I said to him:

"Why should you be serious? You are the happiest man in the world."

He looked at me with his head tilted back a bit in the manner some school teachers assume toward their pupils.

"It is because I have been so happy that I am so serious."

I thought that over for a minute or two, but got nowhere with it.

"Sort of action and reaction, you mean."

"No. I don't think your queer pendulum rule applies to intelligent happiness. I have been so happy all my life that I am afraid when I think of it. I suffered a bit when I was very young, but that little torture could hardly have purchased all the splendor since. I've been the happiest man in the world. I believe I still am—if I dared let myself think about it."

This was a little new to me: a man worried because he was so happy.

"Heaven has given you your happiness: your health, your courage, your gaiety, your philosophy. Accept them. Rejoice."

Again he looked at me. I tempted him with a red-and-white bit of solid, dripping lobster meat. He did not even see the extended fork.

"Heaven has given me many things and I am grateful. But the best gifts heaven has you earn. You buy—." His voice became curiously firm, "I think I'm afraid to pay the price."

Well, I gave up. Here was one of the clever-est youngsters on earth who threw away a fortune such as is given to few, and he was talking about earning and prices.

"You never knew the cost of anything in your life," I said, "nor how to earn it."

He almost leaped at me across the table. "That's it! That's it! I don't realize the cost and I doubt if I could earn it!"

I was through. I told him so. The lobster was tasty. They gave you plenty of melted butter with it. I didn't have to worry about the company—for they were honest plain people who ate there—and I did not have to worry about the conversation for Blue would maintain that if he felt like it, and if he didn't, it would be foolish for me to undertake one. I ate. And ate. And ate.

Blue watched me steadily and I watched him as best I could. I could see his face relax its serious-ness little by little. Finally he burst out laughing. "I almost love you," he said. "You are the most innocent doggonedest glutton I ever saw in my life. I think it's your best virtue. Your others are only compromises."

"Isn't the golden mean the secret of something or other," I parried. I really didn't care. I never bothered over rules invented by philosophers for philosophers.

"Yes," he smiled. "Mediocrity."

I paid the check. Blue made no pretense at it. I'll wager he didn't have twenty cents in all the world. We moved out and up through the deserted market district, by Faneuil Hall, by the Old State House, through Newspaper Row, up over Beacon Hill, and then swung off toward Copley Square. I wanted to take the car at Park Street but he insisted on going with me for a way.

We stopped outside the subway entrance at Dartmouth and Boylston Streets. There was the usual emptiness brooding over Copley Square. One needs bands and fireworks to fill the emptiness of Copley Square at night. Blue stood with me looking over toward the gloomy pile of Trinity Church. He saw nothing, I know. He was in some other world, the abstract World of No Compromises. He certainly was a queer sort, Blue; and never queerer than at that moment: bareheaded, silent, tall, his lips moving now and then, his suit of hemp sagging on his lean frame, a trace of a wrinkle between his eyebrows.... I suppose he was thinking. He was always thinking. But heavens, he was serious that night!

A pretty girl passed, one of those tall slender youngsters who look like schoolgirls in Boston until they are thirty. I have a weakness for pretty girls. I watched her pass and then turned to discover if Blue had seen her. He was looking at me, smiling a little.

"Why don't you get yourself a girl?" I asked him.

He didn't reply.

"Will you please tell me what you want?" I tried again.

Blue was still silent. He began to hunt through the pockets of his clothing—it had pockets—for something or other. He found it, finally. I think it was a breviary. It might have been a prayer book. He went through the pages carefully until he found a tinted religious card. It had a picture on it and a motto. He gave it to me.

Then he turned and slipped along toward the river. I watched him go. I felt sorry for him. Why, I don't know. He was much happier than I was and had more reason to be. I saw him start across Commonwealth Avenue. I read the card. It was a line from the Curate of Ars.

"The cross is the gift God gives his friends."

It is a heroic sentiment, but just where Blue came in I couldn't see. I put it in my pocket, went downstairs, took a Newton car for home, and went to bed.

# Chapter 7

I happened to be in Boston early in November. The nights began to be very cold. Then one day we had the first snow. Boston took the snow very beautifully, as it always does. I was a bit worried about Blue and set out after breakfast to find him. The sight of the gold dome of the statehouse above the white trees of the Common almost made me forget what an incoherent, clique-ridden, unproductive settlement Boston is. Blue is a loyal Bostonian—in spite of his spiritual cosmopolitanism—and so I was careful, when I found him leaving his rooms, not to make any remark of my observations. Once I did repeat to him the cynical observation of a westerner that Boston was chiefly noted nowadays for its mistakes—an observation true, I suppose, of many cities. You can imagine the flow of bizarre indignation that Blue loosed upon me.

Blue was loyal to his city. It was a fine loyalty, and a rare loyalty in America. For it was not the business-booster loyalty, but the loyalty of one who loved the sound and stir of its crowds, who loved its earth and water and walls and trees, who loved its ghosts and memories, who loved it as one loves a family home. Blue was, if ever anyone was, loyal to heaven and home. Home to him was Boston. Although, if you attacked the earth, Blue would have jumped as readily to its defense. He would have told you—as he told me once—that some centuries ago the earth was chosen as the Home of all the universe. He would have stooped down and patted the earth as one pats a pet. He would have told you that the day the earth was sanctified as Home is called Christmas, though it is celebrated now for everything but that. He would have told you—standing, probably, on a street corner, or against a fence or wall—a thousand things, one thing leading to another, and each vivid in its own way, until you were awhirl at the wonder of creation and caught your breath at the sudden strangeness of common places. Blue would probably have you down on your knees to salute, like an Indian, the earth with a kiss. Or he would have you in some nearby church thanking God for the earth. And you would do these things not as a result of any exhortation on his part, but as a sort of easy, natural consequence of having heard him talk. You knew he was absolutely right; though, the next morning—if you were like me— you would have lost much of your enthusiasm and forgotten much of what he said. And you would wonder how a man could be so unique and still be so right.

Blue looked pretty thin. I discovered a little later that he had not been eating well. Poverty in a religious order is one thing, and poverty in the slough of a gold-run city is another. Very few who take vows of poverty have to beg for their next meal or have to sleep out on park benches of bitter nights with an inner jacket of newspapers to hold off Brother Cold. Many a night Blue must have slept with the derelicts of the city in the evil-smelling "hotels" that charity provides for the down-and-outers. And many a morning he must have chopped the city's wood for a miserable breakfast. There were lines on his face I had never observed before, lines that told of the tortures of a sensitive soul. Blue had pledged himself to the service of Lady Poverty, and it was a service that called for a hero. As I walked down Beacon Hill with him that morning, the snow, which had appeared so beautiful to me a few minutes before, took on something of the aspect of an enemy. I can understand the poverty that dwells in cloisters and refectories, but the poverty that strangles one at night when a relentless blizzard is piling up death in the dark slums of a great city is a poverty beyond my affection. But to such poverty Blue went like a man to his lover. He embraced it. That very morning I remarked to him about the two aspects of the snow. His worn face lighted with what I must call a sort of splendor. "All these things can serve my Lady Poverty," he said. "She is a beautiful mistress. She brings not only love but great understanding."

Our views were so completely different that I decided not to argue. Besides, it is difficult to argue with a man when he is talking in a sort of blank verse. But I was worried about Blue with his somewhat nebulous Mistress Poverty facing a winter in Boston. I suggested—timidly, I must confess—that he get himself a job as a janitor in an apartment house. Lodgings usually went with the job, I explained. Blue laughed till his eyes ran with water. "Aha!" he lifted his voice and thrust up his hand in a quick gesture, "My old friend, Mr. Compromiser."

"Your old friend, Reason," I shot back. "At any rate, your old friend Sanity."

He turned to me seriously: "Do you really believe there is so little charity left that I shall be unable to live on it?"

"I don't know how little charity is left, or how much," I explained, "but I do know they find plenty of people starved to death and frozen to death in a merry and pious city like this."

He stared at me as if to learn if I were jesting or not.

"I'm not joking," I answered his look. "If you plan to live on charity this winter in Boston, you had better choose some friend more affluent and helpful than your Lady Poverty."

I thought I had clinched my argument. But it turned out there was no argument. He had his plans all made up and he wasn't debating them with me. He was merely searching for some advance information.

We strode along for a couple of blocks, Blue with his hands in his pockets, his long legs swinging. He was hatless, as usual, with three or four black curls tossing on his forehead. Blue always struck me as being a handsome sort of youngster. Yet I doubt if he ever commanded any particular admiration from women. He was, I suppose, too intensely interested in himself to interest, offhand, any woman. Blue was silent as we went along.

We swung toward the river. We found a sun-warmed bench down a way. Blue turned his dark eyes on me—eyes crammed with dreams and hope and steady courage. "You are a good friend of mine," he said. "I will tell you."

He told me.

Blue, it seems, had found his vocation. That was the way he put it. He was going to pledge himself to poverty and live among the poor. He would give up his attic room and lodge wherever his wandering brought him. He would live with the downtrodden and the shiftless in charitable institutions. He would sleep out on the parks and in the fields when the weather allowed it. He would live in the worst of hovels and the most repulsive of slums. He had been training for this life, he told me. He had been sleeping on the hardest of beds and on the floor. He had been eating little food and the worst kind of food. He had been chumming with outcasts for several months so that he might learn their ways and manners. Now, he said, he thought his novitiate was over. He was ready to go forth, with no name or with any name, to live with the derelicts of modern civilization and bring to them the story that they would never heed elsewhere. And that story? It was, of course, the story of Christ.

Blue's eyes shone as he talked. These brazen souls and weary souls and indifferent souls would never, he maintained, go into a church to pray or listen. They would not go into a mission establishment unless it were for food and sleep, and the preaching they received with their bed and fare they took as a sort of price they paid. They would not stop to heed a street harangue. They would suspect a minister or social worker on sight. But they would listen to him, their companion, their fellow, as they made their listless journeys or lay awake in their haphazard sleeping places.

"Already," said Blue, his voice quivering, "I have two men for converts. They have the stuff of saints, some of these poor fellows. You should see their new courage when I tell them of the providence of God."

So, on and on he went. These derelicts were ill-fits to him, not wastrels, not loafers. I can picture Blue with his fine drawn face and luminous eyes telling them of the loaves and fishes, or of the Master who wept for Lazarus and then raised him from the dead. Blue was confident that in this work lay his career. He hoped, he said, others would someday join him, others who would go into the factories and great offices and teach there, as comrades, by character and example. They would be the Spies of God, he decided. Their unselfishness, their patience, their courage, their amiability, their fine wholesome lives would be living sermons to those who read only the newspapers and disdain the preacher. He even hoped that someday his spies would go into crafts like journalism and advertising and try to win men to a desire for truth and an affection for beauty. And such, briefly, was his great dream of a Secret Service for God.

I cannot—I do not even try to—reproduce the spirit of Blue as he told me of his plan. He talked with his usual intensity, and never did he seem more sure of himself and more right. Listening to him was like listening to some great piece of music. And never have I seen a man happier than he that day.

I was too overcome by the heroism of his vision to offer even one of the hundred practical objections that occurred to me. "Why not?" I said to myself. "Why not?" Indeed, in a sudden surge of desire for a clutch at this glorious destiny, I almost pledged myself to his plan. "Why not?" I kept saying. "Why not?" But caution came with its small whisper: "This isn't normal. Think of your old age...."

Blue was watching me. He knew, I suspected, the conflict in my mind. I leaned over. I wanted to put my arm halfway around his shoulders as one does to young boys. I felt sorry for this great lad alone with his magnificent vision in a world of selfishness fortressed by steel and stone. But I remembered the great prophets who were once as alone as Blue. Great prophets are, I imagine, always, even in their success, alone like Blue.

I said to Blue: "You are certainly in line for that cross you say God gives his friends." That was all I could say.

It was three weeks before I saw Blue again.

There isn't much else to tell of him. I left him by the river that day and went in town to lunch. He didn't want any lunch. He watched me go a little sadly. I believe he expected me to join wholeheartedly with him in his project. Perhaps he thought I would join him there and then. But I had to go along. I was hungry, for one thing. And, for another, I had some business to attend to. Blue had held me spellbound by his magnificent vision. I could see, as he saw, this army of humble men going out into life, pledged to the arduous poverty of those who have no place to lay their heads, winning souls in the intimacy of comradeship, stirring souls by their hard wholesome lives, teaching souls by inexhaustible kindness and unfailing example. I understood his great project: this marvelous body of mendicants, unknown, unidentified, "Spies of God," scattered through the hypocrisy of our lives, in the mines, in the factories, in the offices, in the slums, reaching as no soapbox orator or pamphleteer or newspaper editor or pulpit preacher could, reaching the indifferent, the callous, the wayward. Truly, it was a noble vision. And I really believe Blue could have carried a great deal of it out. He was irresistible personally—when he wanted to be. He had put behind him more of life than even the extraordinary man. He was practical in achieving his own purposes. But his life wasn't the life for me. Business, I believe, is the backbone of our civilization, business regulated and run with the cooperation of science. That, I think, is my vocation. I want to make a great deal of money. I like the good things of life.

I have no calling for the sort of life Blue would wish. I feel that when I can get together some money—fifty million, say—I can do a great deal of good with it. I told Blue this once. He looked at me in that queer way of his for several moments. Then he smiled.

"You have a rare ambition. You are very noble, indeed."

I went to New York for a couple of weeks. I
was away longer than I expected. When I returned
I went to Blue's lodging house on Beacon Hill.
He hadn't been there for ten days. Nobody knew
where he was. Nobody seemed interested.

I felt a strange remorse for my coldness to
him on my last visit. I should have encouraged
him more, I reproached myself. Perhaps, I said
to myself, he has already gone forth to his work
among the poor.

Three days later I received a note from a nurse
at the Boston City Hospital saying that she had
one J. Blue as a patient and that he had asked her
to write to me.

An hour after I found the note, I was in the
hospital.

I did not have to search the ward for Blue's cot.
It was the center of a group: a nurse, two youngsters of about sixteen years, one on crutches, and
an emaciated old man. Blue was raised slightly on
the backrest. I could see as I approached what a
skeleton he was of his former self. But my crowded
fears of the previous hour were dispelled. He was
smiling a smile that had not lost its charm in spite
of the thinness of his face. He was gesticulating with his fine slender hands. Everybody was
laughing with him. The ward had some twenty

cots, about ten on a side, and those who could raise their heads were watching him. I imagine all who could walk were at his bedside. I don't know what he was saying to hold them so enthralled, for he stopped to greet me as I approached. I suppose he had a special way with good common people that he never showed to me. Indeed, I believe he was more at home with these people and happier. The boy in him had a chance to play. And he and they were nearer the wordless understanding that is bred of suffering much.

He smiled up at me: "Have I bothered you? I was afraid you would worry not finding me at my lodging—"

My look stopped him. "Good heavens!" I burst out. "Of all the idiots—"

"I knew it," he interrupted, still smiling. "I knew it. You think this is some stunt of mine. And I'm crazy."

What was the use?

He thought I was going to scold him for being ill in a hospital, as if I thought his being ill were a sort of lark! What I wanted to tell him was that the sight of him was inspiration to me, and courage, and faith. I wanted to tell him that the spectacle of him alive and smiling cleansed me—as it always did—of the cynicism and skepticism that settled like dirt on my mind. Here he was, on his back, worn, thin, brave, smiling, the dream still dominant in his eyes, and here he was hoping he had not "bothered" me.

I couldn't say anything. I took his hand, but the gesture seemed trivial so I dropped it. His group of admirers dispersed. I was left alone with him.

Blue was weak enough. He had had a bad time of it for several weeks. It seems that soon after I left him after our last meeting he found himself a job in a lumberyard. The laborers were mostly derelicts and their boss not much better. They were a hard gang. But Blue got along amazingly well. They liked him and he liked them. In a week he had three or four comrades.

"They were great fellows," Blue explained to me, "really great fellows. I would have had them remembering their souls in no time."

I was skeptical. I said so. The typical city lumberyard gang is a tough lot and not given over to remembering—if they ever heard of—their souls. Blue was a little irritated at me.

"It is because of your attitude that they are very much what they are," he informed me. "You don't know them."

I didn't argue. Didn't Matt Talbot work in a

lumberyard? And I suppose Blue, if he set about it, could have converted the lumber itself.

At any rate, Blue made great progress on his program. He sat up in bed, his eyes glowing, as he told me of his successes. He was afraid at first that these men would not take him into their confidence, that he would not get under their skins. But he had no trouble. In a week they were looking up to him and speaking almost reverently of him when by themselves.

One of those November drizzles, cold, bleak, endless, a common feature of Boston, had wet and chilled the city. Blue had no overcoat and no rubbers or heavy shoes. But he was happy. He was getting, little by little, what he had wanted: the cross God gives his friends. No one ever went searching for it more persistently than Blue.

His sufferings and misfortunes were like successes to you and me. He had everything, but, as he would put it, he had had nothing. "Now," he almost whispered, "I am really making some progress. Pray that I can persevere—"

One of the lumberyard gang was a huge amiable Negro, Joe, who managed to get drunk late every afternoon. Blue, of course, became attached to him. Every night he saw to it that Joe reached home. He lived about four blocks from the yard.

One night, during the disheartening drizzle, he was especially drunk. Blue as usual started home with him. Blue was no Hercules, by a long shot, and this nightly trip, after a grueling day in the yard, drained his energy. But it did not drain his spirit. This night as they were crossing at Dover and Washington Streets—a particularly sordid and crazy corner—Joe reeled, slipped Blue's hold, and fell. A great limousine came shooting out of the traffic, taking advantage of a sudden gap. It was going straight for the prostrate Joe. Blue leaped, grabbed the Negro's head and shoulders, and pulled him back. The driver jammed on foot and hand brakes. The car skidded, swerved on the wet street. Blue stumbled forward. The machine struck. Joe was safe. Blue ended up in the city hospital.

"It was really an act of God," Blue explained.

"Close enough," I agreed.

"No, I don't mean that," he returned. "I mean the whole business. The boys heard about it in the yard, and I am quite a hero—a hero for stumbling in the way of an automobile. But this will help my influence. And then what luck to be here." His eyes roamed around the ward from one human wreck to another. "They are beautiful souls, most of them. It is only in a place like this that one can learn the vast amount of human agony in the world...."

"Suppose you had been killed?" I asked him.

"I think that would have been best of all. I know I am a coward to say that. But this life is so beautiful that I am afraid of it sometimes."

I asked him if he wasn't frightened of death. My question amused him. He was going to take a chance on God's mercy, he said.

"And apart from that," he smiled up at me, "why should I be afraid to do what every coward and scoundrel since the beginning of the world has done?"

So went our conversation. I learned from him with difficulty that he had been seriously hurt.

In his weakened condition, due to under-nourishment as well as the accident, the physician feared pneumonia. None developed and, the nurse told me, they expected he would be able to leave in a week.

Five o'clock came and time to go. Blue waved his thin hand and forearm at me: "Please don't bother coming in again." He was smiling. What could I say?

As I left the ward, there were two visitors arriving. The nurse explained to them that it was after hours. They had just come from work, they argued. She let them in. One was a giant Negro, the other a stocky full-faced white with the nose and ears of a pug. They both were shabby in dirty working clothes and twirled worn hats nervously. They had evidently cleaned and polished up their faces. I knew, of course, whom they were going to see.

You would have thought they were about to interview a king. No yard slavedriver, no burly boss, no owner could, I'll wager, intimidate that pair. Yet, they moved half on tiptoe up to Blue's bed. There was a gentleness, almost an awe, about their walk.

Blue's face lighted up. "Hello, Joe. Hello, Mike," I heard him call. The two shook hands awkwardly with him. Then Mike produced a package from his coat. I couldn't see very well, but I think it was a book, probably a purchase from a Dover Street secondhand shop. It cost them, I suppose, the price of a pint of gin. They sat down.

Blue caught my eye as I loitered in the corridor. I felt embarrassed and went along out.

All that evening and night I could think of little else besides Blue. Here he was, in a hospital, weak, penniless, with a titanic program of heroism mapped out for himself, and here he was grateful for his misfortunes and enthusiastic about the future. I had admired his outline of his work: his Spies of God. I had been moved by the nobility and hardship of his plans. But I never believed he would get anywhere much with them. Yet here he was already making progress. Here he was, happier and braver than ever because heaven had slipped him a large allotment of suffering. If that man was not a living demonstration of faith, no man was.

I had a few minutes the next afternoon and decided to drop in on Blue. I glanced into the ward from the corridor. His cot was empty.

I was surprised at this. The nurse was talking to a tall white-faced man of about fifty. He was nodding his head sagely as she spoke. I disliked his manner immediately.

I could hear the nurse: "...suddenly during the night. Probably an embolus."

The tall man wrinkled his brow with great show of astuteness. "Well," the thin mouth said, "what good end can such fellows come to with their gin and bad companions...."

With that, he turned on his heel and disappeared.

The nurse hesitated before she spoke to me. I caught a strange look on her face. The bottom fell out of my being.

"Not Blue?" I tried to say, but no sound came.

"That man who just went out owned the car that hit him," said the nurse.

My mind was afloat. What car? What man? Hit whom? I turned to her helplessly. I could not articulate. She understood. There was a film of moisture over her eyes. I could not hear. I read her lips:

"Yes, Blue," they said.

All this seems so long ago. It is not quite two years.

This afternoon as I write, the sunlight lies across my desk. There is some quality in it that makes me think autumn is already here. Perhaps it is the pleasant warmth it has when it rests on my hands.

For the life of me I can't believe that Blue is dead. No more could I believe it that day in the hospital. Why should this sunlight be so beautiful, why should people walk up and down the street, why should four robins hop in and out of the tree shade on the lawn beyond my window, why should the glory of autumn be already in the air and still Blue be dead? Why should I be here and Blue be dead? Why should that magnificent soul with his great vocation be gone, and people like me still here, and the girl who waits on me at the German restaurant, and the three fossilized old women with whom I have, now and then, to play bridge, and Scott Jackson, the wealthiest man in the state, and the conductor on the streetcar that just passed…. Why are all of us here and not Blue?

It can't be so. No one so brave, so heroic, so glorious, so immensely above the rest of us can leave us suddenly like that. He can't have gone— Blue and his Spies of God. No. Say what you will. Do what you will. You can't make me believe that Blue is dead.

# Notes on Mr. Blue

by
Stephen Mirarchi, Ph.D.

## ABBREVIATIONS USED IN THE NOTES

*CCC*   *The Catechism of the Catholic Church*, 2nd edition (Rome: Libreria Editrice Vaticana, 1997).

*CE*   All references to the *Catholic Encyclopedia* are to the original edition published from 1907–1912 in New York by Robert Appleton Company in fifteen volumes. This comprehensive reference work is available online at New Advent (www.newadvent.org/cathen), as well as at Catholic Answers (oce.catholic.com).

*CW*   G. K. Chesterton, *The Collected Works*, 37 vols. (San Francisco: Ignatius Press, 1986–2012).

*DR*     All Bible references are to the Douay–Rheims 1899 American edition, unless otherwise noted.

*GG*     F. Scott Fitzgerald, *The Great Gatsby: The Authorized Text*, 1925 (New York: Scribner, 1995).

*JV*     St. John Vianney, *The Spirit of the Curé of Ars*, trans. Alfred Monnin, ed. John Edward Bowden (London: Burns, Lambert, and Oates, 1865).

*OED*     *Oxford English Dictionary Online*, Oxford University Press, September 2015.

# Foreword

2: "The scales of pettiness fall off the soul"

The image of scales falling away is a powerful one in the Bible, signifying God's triumphant healing and renewal in both body and spirit through a mediator. When Ananias obeys God's command and heals Saul, "immediately there fell from his eyes as it were scales, and he received his sight; and rising up, he was baptized"—the spiritual birth of St. Paul (Acts 9:18).

The same language is used in some modern translations when the archangel Raphael obeys God's command and instructs Tobiah in the healing of Tobit's eyes (Tobit 11:7–14 [RSV]).

# Chapter 1

### 5: "Pilgrimage to Tyburn"

The infamous site of public executions from 1196 to 1783, the Tyburn Tree gallows in London saw the cruel deaths of many tens of thousands of felons, including more than 100 Catholic martyrs of the Reformation.

### 5: "Thomas More"

Beatified in 1886, St. Thomas More (1478–1535) was canonized on May 19, 1935. Father of four and chancellor of England under Henry VIII, More was imprisoned and eventually executed for refusing to condone the King's invalid marriage to Anne Boleyn and the King's usurpation of the pope's rightful authority over the Church of England.

In his homily at the canonization Mass, Pope Pius XI highlighted More's love of God even to the utmost sacrifice: "Nor could the tears of his wife and children make him swerve from the path of truth and virtue" (quoted in James Monti, *The King's Good Servant but God's First*, p. 454).

## 5: "Troubadour"

*God's Troubadour: The Story of St. Francis of Assisi*, written by Sophie Jewett, was published in 1910. In his biography of St. Francis, G. K. Chesterton sharply distinguished the troubadour from the jongleur: "when [Francis] and his secular companions carried their pageant of poetry through the town, they called themselves Troubadours. But when he and his spiritual companions came out to do their spiritual work in the world, they were called by their leader the Jongleurs de Dieu" *(CW*, Vol. 2, p. 67).

## 6: "Tonneau"

The back seating area of a car, sometimes open or uncovered. Compare with Nick's description of Gatsby and his "gorgeous car" (*GG*, p. 68), which ends up being one of the key pieces of information Wilson relies on to target Gatsby.

## 10: "Gashouse"

The narrator means "a low-income area," as in a gashouse district (*OED*).

## 11: "Madcap"

"Wildly impulsive," reckless or extravagant (*OED*). Speaking of St. Francis's meeting with St. Dominic, Chesterton writes of St. Francis's extraordinary ability to inspire great generosity in people of every class merely by the force of his personality: "It was a very real victory for the Franciscan spirit of a reckless faith not only in God but in man" (*CW*, Vol. 2, p. 109).

## 11: "In his shirtsleeves"

That is, without his expected suit coat. Compare with Nick's arrival at Gatsby's once Gatsby desires privacy for his adulterous activities with Daisy and has dismissed his former servants (*GG*, pp. 119–120).

## 12: "Boston Common"

The oldest public park in America, the nearly fifty acres of Boston Common were established in 1634.

## 12: "Three burlap bags"

Burlap and sackcloth are roughly synonymous in general usage. Connolly invokes the extreme penitence of dressing in "sackcloth and ashes," such as the residents of Nineveh did in response to Jonah's prophesying (Jonah 3:4–6).

## 12: "Episcopal dean of St. Paul's"

The historic Episcopal Cathedral Church of St. Paul, consecrated in 1820, became the seat of the Episcopal bishop of Massachusetts in 1908. It borders on Boston Common.

## 14: "Lady Poverty"

St. Francis of Assisi (1181–1226) responded to his friends' jabs about his suitability for marriage by saying that he was "about to take a wife of surpassing fairness," Lady Poverty (*CE*, "St. Francis of Assisi"). The Florentine painter Giotto di Bondone (1266–1337) immortalized their nuptials in one of the many elaborate frescos at the Basilica of St. Francis in Assisi, consecrated in 1253. Dante mentions the lovers Francis and Poverty in Canto XI of the *Paradiso*.

Chesterton comments, "St. Francis was talking the true language of a troubadour when he said that he also had a most glorious and gracious lady and that her name was Poverty" (*CW*, Vol. 2, p. 68).

## 15: "Hans Christian Andersen"

Though a prolific novelist and travel writer, Andersen (1805–1875) is best remembered for his more than 150 fairy tales, from "The Little Mermaid" to "The Emperor's New Clothes" and

"The Ugly Duckling." A confirmed Lutheran, Andersen wrote many works with strong Christian themes such as "The Travelling Companion," which presents the burying of the dead as a corporal work of mercy. Connolly would later write the story for the 1952 film *Hans Christian Andersen*, which was nominated for six Academy Awards.

## 16: "His self-sufficiency"

Connolly will develop this concept more fully with the further inclusion of Thoreau later in the novel. Writing of a later stage in St. Francis's spiritual development, Chesterton notes that a "saint is never supercilious, for he is always by hypothesis in the presence of a superior" (*CW*, Vol. 2, p. 107).

## 17: "On his knees"

Speaking to star director Frank Capra at a party in 1929, Connolly tried to push his new friend to stand for something with his films: "Happiness is not just a new suit of clothes...It's getting down on your knees to beg God for mercy, and knowing that He hears you" (Frank Capra, *The Name Above the Title*, p. 121).

# Chapter 2

## 18: "The *Sun* and Frank Munsey"

Frank A. Munsey (1854–1925), newspaper and magazine magnate, made tens of millions of dollars in buying and consolidating publications like the *Sun*. By the early 1920s, Munsey's only rival was William Randolph Hearst. Though Munsey's editorial style was popular, it was inevitably populist. Connolly invokes Munsey right before narrating Blue's rooftop living arrangements, which stand in contrast to Munsey's. To wit, upon Munsey's purchase of "the historic Stewart Building" in Manhattan for $4 million in 1917, "it is reported that it is Mr. Munsey's idea to build a monumental building that will compare favorably with New York's finest office buildings" (*The Bookseller, Newsdealer and Stationer*, November 1, 1917, p. 516).

## 18: "Rockefeller Institute"

John D. Rockefeller Sr. established The Rockefeller Institute for Medical Research in 1901, with formal laboratories opening in 1906, a hospital in 1910, and a doctoral degree-granting school in 1959. Now the Rockefeller University, the institution has had twenty-four Nobel Laureates.

## 19: "Varying degrees of happiness in heaven"

See John 14:2, "In my Father's house there are many mansions. If not, I would have told you: because I go to prepare a place for you." Aquinas quotes this passage and treats the subject in general in Question 93 of the "Supplement" (*Supplementum Tertiae Partis*) to the Third Part of the *Summa*.

## 19: "A tent he could pitch there"

A powerful recurring image in the Bible, pitching a tent shows the establishment by God of a covenant with humanity and its eventual fulfillment in Incarnational abiding, akin to a Catholic tabernacle. See, for instance, Moses as a mediator in such a tent between God and the Israelites (Exodus 33:7), and the opening of the Gospel of John, in which the phrase revealing that Christ "dwelt among us" is translated by some as "pitched his tent" or as the intransitive verb "tabernacled" (John 1:14).

## 20, 23: "Only on stormy nights" / "only on rainy nights"

When Thoreau started his experiment in the woods on July 4, 1845, he noted: "My house was not finished for winter, but was merely a defense against the rain, without plastering or chimney." Thoreau also mentions a previous dwelling: "The only house I had been the owner of before, if I except a boat, was a tent" (*Walden*, "Where I Lived, and What I Lived for").

## 21: "Soldiers marching, all marching"

Connolly's depiction of Blue's fondness for military pomp and processions recalls the once-standard teaching on the distinctions in the communion of Heaven and Earth: the Church Militant, those engaging in the good fight on Earth; the Church Suffering, those undergoing purification in Purgatory; and the Church Triumphant, those rejoicing in Heaven, who continue to intercede for others. See *CE*, "The Church."

## 21: "Glorified circus wagon"

Compare the narrator's description of Blue's packing case to Tom Buchanan's scornful description of Gatsby's car: "'I'll take you in this circus wagon'" (*GG*, p. 128).

## 21: "Pennon"

As Connolly features military imagery in this chapter, the historical definition for pennon—a flag used on a lance by a knight ensign or lancer—is all the more appropriate than a standard synonym for flag (*OED*).

Connolly will draw on Chesterton's definition of a "cosmic patriot" at the beginning of Chapter 7. That same patriot flies a flag out of love for the world: "[The world] is the fortress of our family, with the flag flying on the turret, and the more miserable it is the less we should leave it" (*CW*, Vol. 1, p. 270).

## 23: "Douglaston"

A community in Queens on the north shore of Long Island, Douglaston is only five miles southwest of the Kings Point village in Great Neck—Fitzgerald's West Egg.

## 24: "Chalk disk"

The narrator presumably means a disk-shaped drawing made with chalk, rather than a "chalk disk" ornament, piece of jewelry, or chalk-marking device.

## 26: "Braid and buttons in Harlem"

The expression is both literal—decorative edging material woven into braids alongside fancy buttoning—and figurative: dapper, elegant, formal dress. The Harlem Renaissance was in full swing in 1928.

## 27: "Pinched"

The narrator means to be "subject to a police raid," arrested, or apprehended (*OED*).

## 32: "Destroyers"

The small, fast anti-torpedo boats were relatively new to the U.S. Navy, the first having been commissioned in 1902.

## 32: "Blackwell's Island"

Renamed Roosevelt Island in 1973, Blackwell's is mentioned by Nick as he and Gatsby drive into Manhattan (*GG*, p. 73). Fitzgerald references the Harlem Renaissance with Nick's notice of a limousine "driven by a white chauffeur, in which sat three modish Negroes," who view Nick with "haughty rivalry."

## 32: "Sprawling white conflagrations"

Connolly's figurative use of "conflagration"—a devastating fire of wide scope—is uncommon.

## 33: "One large one shone"

Connolly evokes the Nativity and the Star of Bethlehem; see Matthew 2, for instance. Connolly presents this scene with an implicit understanding of what St. Gregory of Nazianzen wrote in the fourth century, paraphrased by Pope Emeritus Benedict XVI: "At the very moment when the Magi, guided by the star, adored Christ the new king, astrology came to an end, because the stars were now moving in the orbit determined by Christ" (*Spe Salvi* §5).

## 33: "He leaped down"

The Catholic Christmas liturgy has traditionally incorporated in its prayers the reality of Christ, the living Word, leaping down from heaven, as found in the Book of Wisdom: "For while all things were in quiet silence, and the night was in the midst of her course, thy almighty word leapt down from heaven from thy royal throne, as a fierce conqueror into the midst of the land of destruction. With a sharp sword carrying thy unfeigned commandment, and he stood and filled all things with death, and standing on the earth reached even to heaven" (Wis. 18:14–16).

## 33: "My heart would break with all this immensity"

Immensity is one of the standard attributes of God: "By the attribute of immensity we express His transcendent relation to space…To say that God is immense is only another way of saying that

He is both immanent and transcendent" (*CE*, "The Nature and Attributes of God").

## 34: "All matter more"

In St. Augustine's words, "the justification of the wicked is a greater work than the creation of heaven and earth" (*CCC* §1994). Justification, which "establishes cooperation between God's grace and man's freedom…is the most excellent work of God's love made manifest in Christ Jesus and granted by the Holy Spirit" (§§1993, 1994).

## 34: "Bacteria breeding on a pebble in space"

One of Connolly's targets is the materialism taught by American Naturalist writers that reduces human beings to Blue's memorable depiction. Naturalism had surprising endurance as a popular literary form; decades after the publication of *Mr. Blue*, Fr. Harold C. Gardiner, S.J.—longtime Literary Editor of *America* magazine—railed against it in his 1953 essay collection *Norms for the Novel*.

## 35: "Animalcules"

"Any microscopic aquatic organism" (*OED*).

## 35: "I, too, am a Son of God!"

John B. Breslin, S.J., sees "a startling echo of Jay

Gatsby" in this moment that reveals how "Blue and Gatsby clearly serve different Gods" ("The Improbable Career of Mr. Blue," *Boston College Magazine*, Winter 2002).

An even stronger resonance is in Chesterton's description of how St. Francis embodied the man who praises not only creation as it is, but in its *ex nihilo* beginning: "He not only appreciates everything but the nothing of which everything was made…The Franciscan, ragged, penniless, homeless and apparently hopeless, did indeed come forth singing such songs as might come from the stars of morning; and shouting, a son of God" (*CW*, Vol. 2, p. 74–75).

## 36: "His brilliant apostrophe"

In rhetoric, an apostrophe is a turning away from the audience to deliver an exclamation or speech to another person or thing—usually an absent or imaginary one.

# Chapter 3

## 39: "Leaning backward over the city"

Connolly's continual pointing to the "parapet" surrounding Blue's chosen place of residence takes on full meaning as the narrator suspects Blue of imprudence in endangering himself by jumping on top of it. Just as Jesus is tempted on the parapet of the temple (Matthew 4:5; Luke 4:9), is Blue succumbing to a spectacular faith proven only by unnecessary risk? Is he embracing fideism, faith without reason? Connolly's depiction of Blue's singing—and the subsequent "I made a mistake" joke—suggest otherwise.

## 43: "I'll wager a cult"

Blue uses "cult" positively here, as in "a particular form or system of religious worship…directed towards a specified figure" (*OED*).

## 43: "The imitation of Christ"

*The Imitation of Christ* by Thomas À Kempis is a seminal work of Christian ascetic spirituality from the fifteenth century and continues to be one of the most widely read. Speaking of how St. Francis began to attract followers, Chesterton writes: "The adoration of Christ had been a part of the man's passionate nature for a long time past. But the imitation of Christ, as a sort of plan or ordered scheme of life, may in that sense be said to begin here" (*CW*, Vol. 2, p. 61).

## 43: "Christian Science…Mrs. Eddy"

Mary Baker Eddy (1821–1910) was the founder

of the Church of Christ, Scientist, which she established in 1879 after receiving and performing health cures based on her system of Bible-based prayer. Eddy started the *Christian Science Monitor* newspaper, and her church now boasts congregations in seventy countries.

## 44: "One meal a day enough"

Blue echoes Henry David Thoreau, whom he will mention explicitly later: "Instead of three meals a day, if it be necessary eat but one" (*Walden*, "Where I Lived, and What I Lived for").

## 44–45: "He would not, indeed, favor"

See the Letter of James, 2:1–13, for a strong condemnation of the narrator's position. Connolly suggests that Blue is already living in strong relationship with God in whom "there is no respect of persons [partiality]" (Romans 2:11).

## 46: "The animated picture"

Connolly is generally remembered today as a Hollywood producer and screenwriter. Working with Frank Capra officially on films like *State of the Union* (1948), he likely contributed to *Mr. Smith Goes to Washington* (1939) and *It's a Wonderful Life* (1946), though uncredited. Connolly was nominated for an Academy Award for Best Original Screenplay for *Music for Millions* (1944).

### 46: "Delight in children's picture books"

Connolly gives us many examples of Blue's child-like, not childish, joy. "Amen I say to you, unless you be converted, and become as little children, you shall not enter into the kingdom of heaven. Whosoever therefore shall humble himself as this little child, he is the greater in the kingdom of heaven" (Matthew 18:3–4).

### 46: "The fog settling aimlessly over us"

Continuing the image of Blue as a prophet for the times who pitches his tent among us, Connolly invokes the column of cloud or "fog" descending on the roof, just as when Moses saw God face-to-face: "When he was gone into the tabernacle of the covenant, the pillar of the cloud came down, and stood at the door, and he spoke with Moses" (Exodus 33:9).

### 47: "Huge wens"

Connolly plays on the two definitions of wen: a vast, densely populated city; and a skin growth like a wart or cyst.

## 48: "Brutal and consummate efficiency"

In writing Blue's dystopian screenplay, Connolly was at the forefront of a growing body of literature critiquing the rise of the machine-like state that would see its apex in now-classic works like Yevgeny Zamyatin's *We* (1924), Aldous Huxley's *Brave New World* (1932), Arthur Koestler's *Darkness at Noon* (1940), and George Orwell's *1984* (1949). Distinct from typical dystopian visions, Blue's film is eschatological, and Connolly—who mentions Thomas More repeatedly in the novel—likely had More's *Utopia* in mind.

## 53: "His heart bled"

Blue alludes to the longstanding devotion of the Sacred Heart of Jesus, icons of which picture Christ revealing his bleeding heart surrounded by his crown of thorns. The devotion dates to at least the twelfth century, if not farther back (*CE*, "Devotion to the Sacred Heart of Jesus").

## 54: "With the first two fingers"

There is an ancient tradition of making the sign of the cross with two fingers. In the context of a priest's blessing the Eucharistic species, Pope St. Leo IV writes, "Sign the chalice and the host with a right cross and not with circles or with a varying of the fingers, but with two fingers stretched out and the thumb hidden within them, by which the Trinity is symbolized" (quoted in *CE*, "Sign of the Cross").

## 56: "Paean"

Blue uses the word ironically, as it normally means a praising song of thanksgiving, especially for deliverance (*OED*).

## 57: "Clad in their symbols"

Some of these vestments, such as the maniple, may be unfamiliar to readers accustomed only to the *Novus Ordo* or the Ordinary Form of the Mass, generally said in the vernacular, from 1970 onwards. As Blue rightly observes, each vestment has a particular spiritual meaning associated with it, which are preserved in the "vesting prayers" priests say when donning the garments.

The amice is a cloth covering the shoulders and originally the head, and is also called the "helmet of salvation." The alb, a white tunic reaching to the ankles, goes on next and is fastened with the girdle or cincture, similar to a braided cord or belt. A narrow band of material about four feet long, the stole is centered behind the neck on top of the alb, with the ends draping over the chest. The chasuble, worn only by the priest, covers the other vestments as it rests on the chest, shoulders, and back, and is usually beautifully and elaborately decorated, as with a cross like Fr. White's. The maniple is a small loop of fabric worn on the left arm that represents "the cares and sorrows of this earthly life which should be borne with patience in view of the heavenly reward" (*CE*, "Maniple"). See also "Vestments" in *CE*.

## 58: "*In nomine Patris…*"

In the name of the Father, and of the Son, and of the Holy Ghost. Amen.

## 58: "The Mass"

Fr. White has either kept hidden or produced all the necessary elements for the Holy Sacrifice of the Mass. Connolly shows more than a passing knowledge of Catholic liturgy, and Blue's story depends on Fr. White's offering the Mass correctly, with all the proper elements.

The missal is the official liturgical book containing the prayers of the Mass. Unless an altar is portable it contains an altar stone, "a solid piece of natural stone, consecrated by a bishop, large enough to hold the Sacred Host and chalice" (*CE*, "Altar Stone"). The corporal is a cloth placed on the altar and on which the host and chalice are placed, while the cruets are small containers, usually glass, in which water and wine are brought forth. The altar bread must be unleavened. See also "Sacrifice of the Mass" and "Liturgy of the Mass" in *CE*.

### 58: "*Christe eleison*"

"Christ, have mercy"—the middle invocation of the Kyrie, an ordinary part of the Mass.

### 58: "*Credo*"

The Nicene Creed or formal statement of belief, an ordinary part of Solemn Masses.

### 58: "See him turning…*Dominus vobiscum*"

In the Mass of Connolly's time (now often referred to as "the Latin Mass"), the priest offers many prayers *ad orientem*, meaning everyone including himself is facing the high altar. After communicating with God, the priest turns to offer the people what God has offered him. The priest says *Dominus vobiscum*, "the Lord be with you," several times during the Mass.

### 60: "*Qui pridie quam pateretur…*"

"Who, the day before He suffered…"

### 61: "*Hoc est enim corpus meum…*"

"For this is my body…"

## 61: "Then a trumpet peal"

Blue's imagery has basic parallels in the Book of Revelation. See Revelation 8 for the beginning of the successive trumpet blasts.

## 61: "Came Christ"

Fr. White was, through the Mass, bringing Christ truly, really, and substantially to Earth—the Catholic belief in the True Presence of Christ in the Eucharist. However, the "plot twist" in Blue's film is that Fr. White unwittingly brings Christ to Earth for the Final Judgment.

## 61: "Hastening up out of their tombs"

Compare Blue's eschatological vision with the Final Judgment in Revelation: "And I saw the dead, great and small, standing in the presence of the throne, and the books were opened; and another book was opened, which is the book of life; and the dead were judged by those things which were written in the books, according to their works. And the sea gave up the dead that were in it, and death and hell gave up their dead that were in them; and they were judged every one according to their works" (Revelation 19:12–13).

## 62: "I suggested his theology was wrong"

The narrator is correct: Fr. White should be a bishop. Walter Miller's classic work of speculative fiction, *A Canticle for Leibowitz* (1959), accounts for apostolic succession when imagining the launching of a spaceship to bring Catholicism to a new planet. That crew would include "three bishops…They can ordain, and since one of the three is a delegate of the Holy Father, they will even have the power to consecrate bishops" (Walter M. Miller, Jr., *A Canticle for Leibowitz* (New York: HarperCollins, 2006), p. 282).

## 62: "A better insight into the mind of Blue"

Connolly has drawn clear parallels between Blue and White: the lone prophet atop a pinnacle embodying an *alter Christus*—another Christ— amidst a world dominated by mechanistic materialism and pragmatism.

Many Saints speak of a "white martyrdom," a joyful embrace of life's daily struggles to a heroic degree of selflessness. Third century Church Father St. Cyprian of Carthage, for instance, distinguishes "the red martyrdom of blood in times of persecution [from] the white martyrdom of self-sacrificing compassion and acts of charity in times of peace" (Kallistos Ware, *The Inner Kingdom* (Crestwood,

New York: St. Vladimir's Seminary Press, 2000), p. 121–22).

The Irish tradition, dating back to at least the seventh or eighth century *Cambrai Homily*, identifies a threefold martyrdom of white, blue, and red. They are white, "when he separates for sake of God everything he loves, although he suffer fasting or labor thereat;" green or blue, "when by means of them (fasting and labor) he separates from his desires, or suffers toil in penance and repentance;" and red, "endurance of a cross or destruction for Christ's sake" (Whitley Stokes and John Strachan, eds., *Thesaurus Palaeohibernicus*, volume II (Cambridge: Cambridge University Press, 1903), p. 247).

In modern terms, blue "martyrdom is 'to free oneself from evil desires by means of fasting and labor,' pursuing the ascetic way in one's homeland," white martyrdom is , "to 'abandon everything one loves for God's sake,' that is, to accept the vocation of wandering, pilgrimage, voluntary exile for Christ;" and red, "to shed one's blood for Christ" (Ware 122).

Although "blue" is sometimes translated as "green," Charles D. Wright, scholar of Celtic and Anglo-Saxon literature, notes that the *Cambrai Homily*'s threefold martyrdom of white, blue, and red is "a distinction by color that occurs in a variety of Irish and Hiberno-Latin texts" (Charles D. Wright, *The Irish Tradition in Old English Literature* (Cambridge: Cambridge University Press, 1993), p. 74).

Connolly will move Blue into the White martyrdom at the end of Chapter 6.

# Chapter 4

### 64: "Mansard Bank"

Like "Tootsall," "Mansard" is Connolly's invention. In architecture, "mansard" refers to a sloped roof, the bottom of which is steeper—and the narrator has just discovered the roof devoid of Blue.

### 64: "Nitroglycerine"

First constituted or synthesized in 1846, the highly unstable explosive was researched extensively by Alfred Nobel, resulting in his patent for dynamite in 1867. Nitroglycerin (the more common spelling in the U.S.) was already in standard use as a heart medication in the 1880s and saw widespread use in munitions in WWI.

### 66: "A saner man"

The narrator's thoughts on Blue's sanity resonate strongly with similar statements in Chesterton's

*Orthodoxy*. For instance: "People have fallen into a foolish habit of speaking of orthodoxy as something heavy, humdrum, and safe. There never was anything so perilous or so exciting as orthodoxy. It was sanity: and to be sane is more dramatic than to be mad. It was the equilibrium of a man behind madly rushing horses, seeming to stoop this way and to sway that, yet in every attitude having the grace of statuary and the accuracy of arithmetic" (*CW*, Vol. 1, p. 305).

Similarly, Chesterton points out the insanity of Gnosticism and materialism, respectively: "The man who cannot believe his senses, and the man who cannot believe anything else, are both insane, but their insanity is proved not by any error in their argument, but by the manifest mistake of their whole lives. They have both locked themselves up in two boxes, painted inside with the sun and stars; they are both unable to get out, the one into the health and happiness of heaven, the other even into the health and happiness of the earth" (*CW*, Vol. 1, p. 229–30). Perhaps Connolly gave Blue a packing case brightly painted on the outside to contrast with this passage.

## 66: "Dishonest liberal"
The narrator is using the religious sense of the

word, "a person who holds liberal views in theology," not a political one (*OED*).

## 67: "Catechism"

One of the primary methods of teaching the Catholic faith to youth, catechisms are small books in a question and answer format. The now-famous *Baltimore Catechism* had first been issued in 1885. There was a movement in Connolly's time to issue a standardized catechism so that students would need not memorize different wording from the various diocesan catechisms being produced. See *CE*, "Christian Doctrine."

## 67: "Boston's Back Bay"

One of the most affluent areas in Boston to this day, Back Bay is bordered on the north by the Charles River and to the east by the Boston Public Garden (1837). Among its famous destinations is Copley Square, home to Trinity Church (1877) and the Boston Public Library (1895). Mary Baker Eddy's First Church of Christ, Scientist (1895), is nearby.

## 68: "Vows of poverty"

Those entering Catholic religious orders take vows of poverty, chastity, and obedience—simple vows at first, and then solemn. Collectively known as the Evangelical Counsels, they are matters of freedom, not necessity. See *CE*, "Evangelical Counsels."

## 68: "He disliked writing"

Chesterton makes a similar point about St. Francis: "He ignored and in some degree discouraged books and book-learning; and from his own point of view and that of his own work in the world he was absolutely right. The whole point of his message was to be so simple that the village idiot could understand it" (*CW*, Vol. 2, p. 128).

## 68: "Cooperate in this work"

Rather notable is that Connolly writes his narrator as reaching out to others and collaborating with them to tell Blue's story, while Fitzgerald's Nick is a lone wolf who—when trying to gather guests for Gatsby's funeral, for instance—encounters indifference or aversion.

## 69: "Others can be"

Blue's sayings follow a pattern reminiscent of Christ's Beatitudes (Matthew 5:3–10) and Woes (Luke 6:20–26).

## 70: "Life gives you"

Blue's meditation might remind modern readers of St. John Paul II's "Law of the Gift," which he taught in many places: "Christ teaches us that the best use of freedom is charity, which takes concrete form in self-giving and in service" (*Redemptor Hominis* §21).

## 71: "Christian culture"
Connolly gives voice to a concern that has only deepened in modern times. See George Weigel's *Letters to a Young Catholic* (New York: Basic Books, 2004), especially the first chapter.

## 71: "Hotel Ganymede"
The "Union Ganymede" in Connolly's time was a club or "friendly society" for Hotel and Restaurant employees. They would advertise their social events in trade papers like the *New York Hotel Record*.

## 72: "Forever restless"
Compare Blue's virtuous restlessness, which does not settle for natural happiness, with the depraved restlessness Nick criticizes in the Buchanans. For instance, Nick introduces Tom as looking about his property with "his eyes flashing about restlessly" (*GG*, p. 12).

## 72: "Die on Saint Helena"

Napoleon Bonaparte was exiled to the remote island of St. Helena in the South Atlantic Ocean in 1815. He apparently requested a Catholic chaplain in his exile and received one, dying there six years later. See *CE*, "Napoleon I (Bonaparte)."

Blue will mention St. John Vianney later. The Saint mentions Napoleon as a model of courage who inspired his soldiers to take risks they never would on their own. Vianney then writes, "Let us do the same; let us follow our Lord [in taking up our crosses], who has gone before us" (*JV*, "Catechism on Suffering," p. 118).

## 73: "Columbus"

Christopher Columbus, a fervent Catholic, was widely seen in Connolly's time as "unquestionably a man of genius...His success in overcoming the obstacles to his expeditions and surmounting the difficulties of his voyages exhibit him as a man of unusual resources and of unflinching determination" (*CE*, "Christopher Columbus").

## 73: "Joan of Arc"

St. Joan of Arc had just been canonized in 1920 by Pope Benedict XV. Mark Twain's biography of her praised Joan's heroic virtues: "She was of a dauntless courage when hope and courage had perished in the hearts of her nation" (*Personal Recollections of Joan of Arc*, "Translator's Preface"). In the same preface Twain mentions Napoleon but ranks Joan above him.

## 73: "Live snugly"

Blue is echoing *via negativa* Thoreau's famous line about why he went to the woods: "to live deliberately" (*Walden*, Chapter 2).

## 73: "Wrapping paper"

Probably not synonymous with "gift wrap," the likely meaning here is "a special make of strong paper for packing or wrapping up parcels," such as might now be termed packing paper (*OED*).

## 73: "Through suffering"

Connolly has Blue use similar ideas to Christian mystics, those whom Christ invites to share in His redemptive sufferings in a most intimate way for the salvation of souls. Evelyn Underhill's now-classic *Mysticism: A Study of the Nature and Development of Man's Spiritual Consciousness* had been published in 1911.

Blue will mention St. John Vianney later. Compare many lines in his "Catechism on Suffering," such as, "In order to get to heaven, we must suffer" (*JV*, p. 118).

## 74: "Nonconformists"

The narrator voices a standard objection to Transcendentalist writers such as Ralph Waldo Emerson, whose famous essay "Self-Reliance" urges nonconformity.

## 75: "Xavier is home"

Blue's catalog, mostly of Saints, tells us something of what he admires and imitates in God's closest friends. St. Francis Xavier, S.J., is Patron of the Missions, and the "Little Flower" St. Thérèse of Lisieux had just been pronounced co-Patroness of the Missions in 1927. St. Teresa of Avila ("the older Teresa"), great mystic, was also known for her wit. St. Thomas Aquinas and Francisco Suárez were both highly gifted systematic philosophers and held different understandings on such complex topics as natural law. The "Good Thief," traditionally referred to as St. Dismas, reformed his life on the cross next to the crucified Christ and was promised immediate entrance into heaven by the same—a deathbed conversion, as it were (Luke 23:39–43). St. John Vianney begins his "Catechism on Suffering" by speaking of the merits of the good thief (*JV*, p. 113).

## 75: "Tavern at the End of the World"

Blue alludes to Chesterton's 1906 biography of Charles Dickens, which ends with this sentence: "And all roads point at last to an ultimate inn, where we shall meet Dickens and all his characters; and when we drink again it shall be from the great flagons in the tavern at the end of the world" (*CW*, Vol. 15, p. 209).

## 76: "Few intimates"

The narrator's distinction between wide friendship and narrow intimacy has Scriptural echoes, such as Christ's words to his Apostles at the Last Supper: "And you are they who have continued with me in my temptations" (Luke 22:28).

## 78: "Roxbury, Massachusetts"

The neighborhood Connolly grew up in, and one of the original villages in the Massachusetts Bay Colony, Roxbury was founded in 1630. Two strategic strongholds at Fort Hill played roles in the Revolutionary War, and Roxbury later became a suburb of Boston proper in 1868.

In Connolly's time, Roxbury—along with nearby Dorchester—was home to neighborhoods that housed "the largest Jewish community in New England" (Jonathan D. Sarna, ed., *The Jews of Boston* (New Haven: Yale University Press, 2005), p. 154).

## 78: "In terms of eternity"

Though he says it in exasperation, the narrator alludes to the anagogical aspect of Blue's spiritual vision. The Church has taught the anagogical sense of Scripture since at least the thirteenth century: "We can view realities and events in terms of their eternal significance, leading us toward our true homeland" (*CCC* §117–118).

## 79: "Bigotry"

Connolly's portrayal of Blue's absolute intolerance of bigotry—and the narrator's awareness thereof—staves off any wariness modern readers may have about the author's approach to Jewish characters. Additionally, Connolly is indicting Fitzgerald's too-acquiescent narrator Nick Carraway, who, for instance, says nothing when Myrtle's sister Catherine announces that she "almost married a little kyke" (*GG*, p. 38).

## 80: "The world and the flesh…the devil"

In speaking of the world, the flesh, and the devil, Blue cites "the three traditional sources of temptation" (Peter Kreeft, *Angels (and Demons)* (San Francisco:

Ignatius, 1995), p. 121). In his 1933 biography of Aquinas, Chesterton writes that "good things, like the world and the flesh, have been twisted by a bad intention called the devil" (*CW*, Vol. 2, p. 485).

## 81: "Says the song"

This reference is obscure.

## 84: "Capacity for laughter"

Compare with the final line of Chesterton's *Orthodoxy* (1908): "There was some one thing that was too great for God to show us when He walked upon our earth; and I have sometimes fancied that it was His mirth" (*CW*, Vol 1, p. 366).

## 85: "Despite the psalm"

Perhaps Blue has in mind Psalm 98 (97 in *DR*), with its "Sing ye to the Lord a new canticle" opening. Verses 8–9a read, "The rivers shall clap their hands, the mountains shall rejoice together / At the presence of the Lord."

## 85: "The stars are steadfast"

Blue's thoughts on Thoreau recall Emerson's meditation on solitude and the stars: "But every night come out these preachers of beauty, and light the universe with their admonishing smile"

(*Nature*, Ch. 1). Connolly will allude later to the stars as "spies of God."

## 85[†]: "M. C."

The narrator signs his plea to his readers to send him information on Blue with these initials, which of course are those of Myles Connolly—though the narrator is never officially named.

## 86: "'Doing' the lodger's room"

The narrator is highlighting Mrs. Murphy's dialect. Her expression means "to do work upon or at, repair, prepare, clean, wash, keep in order," such as one would expect of a longtime lodging house manager (*OED*).

## 86: "Consumption"

An early word for tuberculosis, consumption refers to diseases that manifest as the wasting away or "extreme weight loss" of the body (*OED*). Tuberculosis was such a public health threat that a specific center, the Boston Consumptive Hospital, was opened in 1906 and expanded rapidly on a 51-acre site in the Mattapan neighborhood, south of Dorchester and Roxbury. A widely held belief at the time was that clean, fresh air could alleviate symptoms or hasten a cure—thus, the bucolic setting.

## 86: "Melt the heart of a wheelbarrow"

The Irish expression "you charm the heart of a wheelbarrow" is said to one whose singing is disagreeable or out of tune (Elizabeth Mary Wright, *Rustic Speech and Folk-lore* (London: Oxford, 1913), p. 166). Mrs. Murphy seems to mean that Blue had no talent for wheedling—or, in a backhanded way, that his smile was genuine.

## 87: "Companylike"

Dialect meaning friendly, affable, comfortable, at home—worthy of good company.

## 88: "A successful column"

Nathanael West's *Miss Lonelyhearts*, which came out in 1933, had exactly that premise at the center of its plot, except with a satiric twist. Like Connolly, West became a denizen of Hollywood, and his book *The Day of the Locust* (1939) is generally recognized as one of the great fictional treatments of that film industry. Both men had film credits in 1937: West, for the story and the screen play (co-written) of *It Could Happen to You*; Connolly, for the story of *It Happened in Hollywood*.

## 88: "Fancies"

Blue means here invented images different from

pious representations like holy cards yet not permanent ideals to be saved for prayer. If the Romantic imagination "is the power of giving to ideal creations the inner consistency of realities" (*OED*), then Blue's "fancies" are the fruit of his sacred or prayerful imagination—a means for him to connect with mothers, or to understand the value of joyful, humble, daily work.

## 89: "Their Calvary"

Mary's standing beneath the Cross of Christ with the Apostle John (John 19:25–27) has been the basis for much sacred art, especially the heart-rending "*Stabat Mater*" poem and hymn. In the Latin Mass, the "*Stabat Mater*" is the Sequence for the Feast of the Seven Sorrows of Mary and is currently optional for the Ordinary form Feast of Our Lady of Sorrows.

## 89: "Hilary Pepler"

A close friend and working partner of Chesterton and Hilaire Belloc, Pepler (1878–1951) converted to Catholicism in 1916. He established St. Dominic's Press, which became famous for the quality of its printing and the work of its artists, among them David Jones (1895–1974), Desmond Chute (1895–1962), and Eric Gill (1882–1940).

The press had among its authors both Jacques and Raïssa Maritain, two of the twentieth century's most important French Catholic intellectuals.

The poem Blue recites, "The Milkmaid," was first published as a broadside in 1923. In 1926, Pepler published it in the eight-page book *The dressmaker; and, Milkmaid*, and more substantially in *Pertinent and Impertinent: An Assortment of Verse* (Ditchling [England]: St. Dominic's Press, 1926), pp. 15-16.

Blue quotes stanzas one and three, with two variations: "the" in Blue's line 4 is originally "her" in Pepler; Blue's "sing" in line 6 is "sings" in Pepler's line 10. Given the rarity of Pepler's book and the importance of the poem to Blue's Mariology, the poem is worth reprinting in full. "Housel" in line 24 means "the consecrated elements of the Eucharist, especially the bread" (OED).

## The Milkmaid

*Our Lady was a Milkmaid,*
*a peasant girl, and poor,*
*she whom Almighty God obeyed*
*would scrub her dairy floor.*

*And meek would goat or heifer stand*
*for Mary in the field,*

*obedient udders to her hand*
*did their abundance yield.*

*Our Lady well could merrimake*
*and sings sweet songs to Him,*
*of butter, cheese, and curdle cake,*
*of how to milk and skim.*

*Though sun and moon or tallow dip*
*threw shadows on the wall*
*the Light she carried on her hip*
*was brighter than them all.*

*And for the fire to cook God's food*
*she gathered fallen sticks*
*among proud trees where grew the Rood,*
*and loomed the Crucifix.*

*Our Lady milled, mixéd the flour*
*with water from the well,*
*the Bread God broke in His last hour*
*to make His first Housel.*

\*       \*       \*

*So sing we songs of bread and bake*
*of butter, cheese, and curdle cake,*
*of wells and washing days;*
*for every Milk Maid's song is blest*

*because one maid with Child at breast*
*has sung them in His praise.*

## 90: "His sister who was ill"

The story is reminiscent of Our Lady of Guadalupe's appearance to St. Juan Diego, who was taking care of a sick relative and was called a familiar name by Mary. Blue will mention her explicitly later.

## 91: "You who stand between me"

Blue's Mariology is still developing at this stage in his spiritual life, which occurs eight to ten years before the present narrative time in this chapter, given Mrs. Murphy's memory of Blue's lodging with her just "after the war," and the narrator's later statement of writing about two years after the events. Blue echoes writers quoted by St. Alphonsus Liguori in his *The Glories of Mary, Mother of God*: "Blosius figures Mary to us, as the only refuge of those that have incured [*sic*] the divine indignation...no one fears to approach her...Mary presents herself between God and his offending creature, and no person is so fit, says St. Bonaventure, to avert the sword of Divine wrath and indignation" (*The Glories of Mary* (Dublin: John Coyne, 1833), p. 87).

## 92: "I do wish someone"

Blue's heartfelt desire is fulfilled in the narrator's writing of the book, which would not be possible without Mrs. Murphy's keeping the letter (all the more extraordinary since she considers him "useless"), Blue's inspiration in writing the letter in the first place, and so on. As this passage occurs in the context of Mary as Mediatrix of Grace, Connolly seems to be asking the reader to consider literature as a means of connecting the horizontal and vertical axes of mediation.

# Chapter 6

## 94: "The Newtons"

About ten miles west of Back Bay, Newton is a picturesque city in the Boston suburbs. The twin lakes are the Waban Hill Reservoir (1876), just northwest of Boston College, and the much larger, famed Chestnut Hill Reservoir (1870), due east of the college.

## 94: "Gothic tower"

Having worked for decades to be formally recognized, Boston College was officially established in 1863 and remains one of the preeminent Jesuit institutions of higher learning. The "Gothic tower" is that of Gasson Hall's, a 200-foot bell tower opened in 1913 whose design is generally credited for the advent of the "Collegiate Gothic" architectural style. Connolly graduated from Boston College in 1918.

## 95: "No stone is left"

Blue is loosely quoting Mark 13:2: "Seest thou all these great buildings? There shall not be left a stone upon a stone, that shall not be thrown down." The phrase "stone upon a stone" such as Blue paraphrases is atypical in English Bible translations; the standard is "one stone upon another." The 1599 Geneva and the 1899 Douay-Rheims use the non-standard translation, as do a few obscure versions such as the 1890 Darby and 1898 Young's Literal.

## 95: "Lost Cause that is never lost"

Speaking of the Irish, particularly the John Redmond Nationalists, Chesterton writes in "The Mistake of Ireland" (from 1919's *Irish Impressions*) that "if theirs is a lost cause, it is wholly worthy of a land where lost causes are never lost" (*CW*, Vol. 20, p. 151). It is worth repeating that Connolly could not have been more proud of his Irish heritage.

## 95: "The Mongol and the Saracen"

Blue probably refers to the thirteenth century

Mongol invasion of Europe, which several Popes sought to repel, including by crusade. The history of Saracen or Muslim Arab conflicts with Christians is complex and longstanding; Blue probably means the infamous ninth century "sack of Rome" as well as Catholic efforts to regain lands and holy items from Saracens in the crusades.

## 96: "Burlesque"

Blue means an unintentionally ridiculous imitation, not an intentional caricature (*OED*).

## 97: "Rhetoric"

A traditional study of the techniques that bring out language's persuasive power, rhetoric follows grammar and logic in the classical *trivium* liberal arts curriculum. In Jesuit education, rhetoric has developed into *eloquentia perfecta*, the process of learning to express oneself well in oratory (public speaking) and writing. The modern reader may catch the prophecy in Connolly's depiction of the narrator, who believes that rhetoric has primacy over personal, lived witness.

## 97: "The Woolworth Building"

When it was completed in 1913, the 60-story Woolworth Building in downtown Manhattan was the world's tallest building designed for human occupancy. Its Neo-Gothic architecture earned it the title of "cathedral of commerce" and set a standard for future skyscraper design.

## 97: "The Bush Terminal Building"

Also known as the Bush Tower, the 29-story office building in midtown Manhattan was completed in 1917. Praised for its interior and exterior Gothic elements, the building is most notable for its narrow base and panel-effect sides. One writer calls it "a razor blade of the Gothic, one long soaring rise of medieval elements combining into a single vertical" (Christopher Gray, "A Skinny Gothic Tower Is to Get a Modern Partner," *New York Times*, April 21, 2002, p. 7).

## 97: "Huskies"

Muscular, strong men "whose appearance suggests strength and force" (*OED*). Since Blue has a penchant for poetry, he may be thinking of Carl Sandburg's "Ready to Kill" from 1916's *Chicago Poems*. The anti-war poem celebrates the blue-collar work ethic of the common man, especially he who provides food, shelter, and clothing for others: "After the farmer, the miner, the shop man, the factory hand, the fireman and the teamster /

Have all been remembered with bronze memorials, / Shaping them on the job of getting all of us / Something to eat and something to wear, / ... And show the real huskies that are doing the work of the world, and feeding people instead of butchering them" (lines 7–10, 14).

## 97: "Pentecostal ardor"

Pentecostal Christians were thriving in Connolly's time. Two such denominations were the Assemblies of God, founded in Topeka, Kansas, in 1901 by Charles F. Parham, and the Church of God in Christ, established by C. H. Mason in 1907. The Asuza Street mission in Los Angeles, headed by William J. Seymour, ran an exuberant, zealous ministry from 1906–1908, the effects of which were "carried to all parts of the country" (Sydney A. Ahlstrom, *A Religious History of the American People*, 2nd ed. (New Haven: Yale, 2004), p. 820).

Crucial to the early Pentecostal theology was the reception of the fullness of the Holy Spirit, two fruits of which were speaking in tongues and supernatural healing, ordinarily while the congregation was assembled. Such moments of witness were highly emotional and passionate—part of the famed "ardor" to which Blue refers.

## 98: "Oratorical"

In light of the narrator's earlier comment about rhetoric, his characterization of Blue's speaking suggests that Blue has some eloquence himself; the question would be where he learned it.

Given that Blue's speech centers on religion's engagement with his times, it is hard not to hear Connolly playing on "oratorical" as "of the Oratory," the Roman Catholic "society of priests… whose purpose was to preach in a plain style to uneducated congregations." Additionally, Connolly introduced Blue's oratory, "a small chapel or shrine in or attached to a house," early in the book (*OED*).

## 98: "Christ on the Thames"

Blue refers to Francis Thompson's poem "The Kingdom of God," whose last two lines are, "And lo, Christ walking on the water / Not of Gennesareth, but Thames!" Thompson (1859–1907) was a celebrated poet, the author of the beloved, mystical poem "The Hound of Heaven," which continues to be included in the Roman Catholic breviary. In his 1913 *The Victorian Age in Literature*, Chesterton praised Thompson for his "sky-scraping humility, his mountains of mystical detail, his occasional and unashamed weakness, his sudden and sacred blasphemies" and dubbed him a "shy volcano" (*CW*, Vol. 20, p. 509, p. 441).

## 98: "The Hudson or the Charles"

These two prominent rivers of Manhattan and Boston, respectively, have featured in the main settings of the novel so far.

## 98: "Boy at Guadalupe and a girl at Lourdes"

Our Lady of Guadalupe appeared in 1531 to 57-year-old St. Juan Diego near Mexico City; Blue apparently means he still had the faithful heart of a boy. St. Juan Diego afterwards lived in a hermitage at the foot of Tepeyac hill, where Mary appeared. In 1666, a team investigating the authenticity of the *tilma* found that the environmental conditions ought to have long decayed the fabric, for the hermitage "borders the north side of a lake, thus receiving on its south side the constant humid air very closely" (quoted in Eduardo Chávez, *Our Lady of Guadalupe and Saint Juan Diego: The Historical Evidence* (Lanham, MD: Rowman & Littlefield, 2006) p. 26).

Our Lady of the Immaculate Conception appeared in 1858 to 14-year-old St. Bernadette Soubirous in an abandoned grotto near Lourdes, France. The majestic Gave de Pau River is just to the north.

## 99: "Out of the union is born their art"

Blue rather provocatively suggests a nuptial relationship between the artist and his age, with art as the fruit of the intercourse. Catholicism has long maintained the nuptial character of the relationship between God and His creation, between heaven and earth. See *CE*, "Mystical Marriage." Chesterton uses a similarly suggestive image to describe the risky adventure of orthodox, historical Christianity in the world: "In my vision the heavenly chariot flies thundering through the ages, the dull heresies sprawling and prostrate, the wild truth reeling and erect" (*CW*, Vol. 1, p. 306). It is worth noting that in the same passage, Chesterton calls Christian Science an "obvious and tame...fad" and rather humorously ranks it alongside Gnosticism as a heresy.

## 99: "Saint Patrick's Cathedral"

Opened in 1879 and completed in 1910, St. Patrick's Cathedral is the seat of the Catholic Archbishop of New York and is widely considered a Gothic masterpiece. The patronage of St. Patrick reflected the growing numbers of Irish Catholics in the diocese.

## 99: "Cathedral of Saint John the Divine"

Though its cornerstone had been laid in 1892, the

Episcopal Cathedral would not be completed until 1941. Blue's "blundering" comment probably refers both to the mishandling of the Cathedral's construction and to its hodgepodge of Gothic and Romantic architectural styles (making it an "anomaly").

## 99: "Mammon"

From the Aramaic, the New Testament Greek word broadly means wealth or riches, but with the connotation that one places one's trust in them (*Strong's Concordance* §3126). Thus, Jesus direly warns, "You cannot serve both God and mammon" (Matthew 6:24).

## 100: "Munificence"

The classical virtue that "disposes one to incur great expenses for the suitable doing of a great work," munificence falls under the moral virtue of fortitude and is distinct from patience, magnanimity, and perseverance (*CE*, "Virtue").

## 100: "Dryness and dullness"

Both of these words have long been used in the Catholic tradition to speak of spiritual states.

Dryness or aridity refers to a state of purgation in which sense experience is no longer consoling; one passes through the desert of the senses, as it were. Dryness can be positive or negative: positive, if one is in a state of grace and the aridity is a rewarding preparation for a higher spiritual state; negative, if one has overindulged in sense experience or has been negligent thereof, bringing on dryness as a consequence (see *CE*, "Mystical Theology"). Blue's use of it is critical: modern artists have overemphasized the Gothic and have neglected their own age.

In the *Summa*, Aquinas distinguishes dullness from blindness: "dullness of sense in connection with understanding denotes a certain weakness of the mind as to the consideration of spiritual goods; while blindness of mind implies the complete privation of the knowledge of such things" (II-II, q. 15, a. 2).

## 101: "Vainglorious"

Generally understood as a product of the vice of pride, vainglory is a distortion of the proper pursuit of glory and can happen in three ways: by seeking glory "for that which is unworthy of glory;" by seeking it from someone "whose judgment is uncertain;" and/or by seeking it with an intention that "does not refer the desire of his own glory to a due end" (*Summa* II-II, q. 132, a. 1).

## 101: "Street car"

The BERY or Boston Elevated Railway Company had absorbed the West End Street Railway's streetcar system by the end of 1897. With the increasing popularity of automobiles, Boston's downtown was often backed up for blocks with electric streetcars and autos; the soon-to-come subway would alleviate much of the congestion.

## 101: "Beacon Street"

A well-traveled road, Beacon Street connects Boston and Newton and borders the Chestnut Hill Reservoir on the south.

## 101: "An old oyster house"

Ye Olde Union Oyster House opened in 1826 and continues to this day. Daniel Webster (1782–1852), the great American statesman and Massachusetts Senator, was a regular.

## 102: "But the best...you earn"

Blue is avoiding the error of Quietism, which advocates completely passive reception of God's grace. However, his phrasing here is dangerously close to the error of Semi-Pelagianism, which posits that "nature and its works [have] a certain claim to grace" (*CE*, "Semipelagianism"). His explosively joyful reaction to the narrator's suggestion a few moments later—"I doubt if I could earn it!"—is closer to the orthodox doctrine of grace as a completely gratuitous gift of God's mercy necessary "for all meritorious acts" (*CE*, "Controversies on Grace"). See also *CE*, "Actual Grace" and "Sanctifying Grace."

## 103: "Doggonedest glutton"

Blue's superlative adjective is an expression of surprise, a half-serious admonishment of his friend's reprobate behavior, and an appropriate spiritual joke, since the sin of gluttony could merit one Hell and "doggoned" has its etymological roots in "God damn" (*OED*).

Blue's use of "virtue" in the next sentence is ironic: gluttony is a vice, but the narrator's dedication to eating has something of the virtuous in it, if only that he eats without compromises.

## 103: "The golden mean"

In Aristotle's ethics, "every ethical virtue is a condition intermediate between two other states, one involving excess, and the other deficiency" (*Stanford Encyclopedia of Philosophy*, "Aristotle's Ethics: The Doctrine of the Mean"). See also the subsection "mean of virtues" in *CE*, "Virtue."

## 104: "Fanueil [*sic*] Hall"

Connolly's original text contains the above typo, which has been corrected in this edition.

Just south of the Union Oyster House lies Faneuil Hall (1741), the site of the great town hall meetings that led to the American Revolution. Even today, hundreds of new citizens are sworn in there every month.

The Old State House (1713) is southwest of Faneuil Hall. It boasts the very balcony from which the Declaration of Independence was first read in 1776.

A frenetic site of political, legal, financial, and of course journalistic activity, Boston's Newspaper Row was home in Connolly's time to at least five major news corporations, including the *Boston Globe* and the *Associated Press*. The narrator and Blue are walking southwest along Washington Street toward Milk Street, the borders of Newspaper Row.

Due west of Faneuil Hall, Beacon Hill is an exclusive neighborhood dating back to at least 1798, when the Massachusetts State House at the top of the hill was completed. The narrator mentions its "gold dome" later.

## 104: "Trinity Church"

Opened in 1877, the Episcopal-affiliated Trinity Church was designed in the form of a Greek Orthodox cross and incorporates Romanesque architectural elements as well.

## 104: "World of No Compromises"

The modern reader may be reminded of Pope Emeritus Benedict XVI's encyclical *Spe Salvi*, in which he observes that "in the concrete choices of life," most people's "openness to truth, to love, to God…is covered over by ever new compromises with evil—much filth covers purity, but the thirst for purity remains and it still constantly re-emerges from all that is base and remains present in the soul" (§46). Benedict does affirm that there "can be people who are utterly pure," just as "there can be people who have totally destroyed their desire for truth and readiness to love" (§45).

## 105: "Breviary"

A portable book containing the prayers of the Divine Office or Liturgy of the Hours, a breviary is specific to a rite (such as the Roman Breviary for the Roman Rite) and is usually issued in multiple volumes keyed to the liturgical seasons, such as Lent/Easter, Advent/Christmas, and Ordinary Time. Though learning how to use a breviary takes time due to its intricacy, it does lay out the specific

Psalms to be prayed daily, as well as the common prayers, Scriptures, and Traditional texts (e.g., writings of Saints, sacred hymns) proper to the particular season or the Saint, feast, or celebration of the day. The Divine Office is obligatory for priests and religious brothers and sisters, with some exceptions, and is ordinarily prayed in common. Many laypeople pray the Office. An English-only translation, as opposed to a side by side English/Latin version, was published in 1879.

## 105: "Curate of Ars"

St. John Vianney (1786–1859), priest of Ars, France, was canonized in 1925 and proclaimed Patron of Parish Priests the year after *Mr. Blue* was published. Blue is using a slightly different translation than that of Monnin's: "The Cross is the gift that God makes to His friends" (*JV*, "Catechism on Suffering," p. 121).

## 105: "Newton car"

The narrator is using the Copley Square subway entrance, opened in 1914; by specifying "Newton car" he distinguishes among the many destinations offered by the streetcar lines.

# Chapter 7

## 106: "The cynical observation of a westerner"

It is difficult not to hear a criticism of Nick Carraway here, who in a couple key places characterizes the East by its missteps. "When I came back from the East last autumn I felt that I wanted the world to be in uniform and at a sort of moral attention forever," he says in the novel's opening pages (*GG*, p. 6). Bookending this, he speaks in the book's final pages of the main characters as "all Westerners" and imagines a drunk woman being carried on a stretcher by "four solemn men in dress suits" who bring her to the wrong address. "No one knows the woman's name, and no one cares. After Gatsby's death the East was haunted for me like that" (*GG*, pp. 184, 185).

## 107: "The loyalty of one who loved"

Connolly alludes through the narrator to Chesterton's definition of the patriot, as distinct from the optimist and the pessimist: "The point is not that this world is too sad to love or too glad not to love; the point is that when you do love a thing, its gladness is a reason for loving it, and its sadness a reason for loving it more" (*CW*, Vol. 1, p. 270). This sentence in *Orthodoxy* comes immediately after the "fortress and flag" line; see "pennon" in the Chapter 2 notes.

## 108: "Slough"

Like John Bunyan's famous Slough of Despond in *Pilgrim's Progress*, a slough is impassable ground due to mud or swamp-like conditions. The narrator is also playing off the figurative sense of its other definition: the wealth of Boston has cast off, like a second skin or slough, those who must live in such places.

## 108: "Brother Cold"

The narrator is playing somewhat mockingly on St. Francis of Assisi's mystical habit of treating every creature, every creation, as a brother or sister—famously, for instance, relegating Mother Nature to Sister, thereby avoiding pantheism yet maintaining the familial relationship.

Chesterton recounts the story of Francis's response to eye surgery in his time. As they were about "to burn his living eyeballs with a red-hot iron," Francis implored, "Brother Fire, God made you beautiful and strong and useful; I pray you be courteous with me" (*CW*, Vol. 2, p. 86).

## 109: "Mistress"

Blue's use of the word is multi-faceted. The narrator emphasizes "service" in the sentence beginning "Blue had pledged himself," so the immediate

meaning of mistress is "a woman who employs others in her service; a woman who has authority over
servants." However, that usage historically hasn't
been spiritual; in Irish English, mistress means
a wife, which reminds us of St. Francis's nuptials
with Lady Poverty (see note under Chapter 1).
Additionally, two meanings obsolete by the early
eighteenth century classify a mistress as "a female
patron or inspirer of an art, religion, [or] way of
life," and a woman or "goddess…regarded as a pro-
tecting or guiding influence" (*OED*).

## 110: "Advance information"

The narrator means that Blue was feeling him
out: testing him or trying to find out what he
thinks before deciding whether or not to reveal his
plan. Even though the narrator could hardly dis-
agree more with him, Blue tells him because "you
are a good friend of mine" (p. 111).

Connolly has used a Biblical inversion here. Jesus
tells a parable of one friend who calls on another in
the middle of the night asking for bread; initially,
the man already in bed refuses. But, says Jesus, "Yet
if he shall continue knocking, I say to you, although
he will not rise and give him, because he is his
friend; yet, because of his importunity, he will rise,
and give him as many as he needeth" (Luke 11:8).

The lesson is about the need to persevere in prayer. Connolly has presented this teaching in reverse: Blue has been completely steadfast with the narrator throughout the book, with no apparent change, and even with resistance. Yet, Blue gives the narrator the "bread" he is looking for—the chance to take up a more rewarding and Incarnational vocation—out of friendship. And it almost works: "In a sudden surge of desire for a clutch at this glorious destiny, I almost pledged myself to his plan. 'Why not?' I kept saying" (p. 113).

## 110: "Hatless"

The early twentieth century gentleman of the great American and European cities would never appear hatless in public unless he wished to flout social mores or he were completely oblivious to basic customs. As a late nineteenth century book of historically-based etiquette instruction for Americans observed, "When the great Beau Brummell was asked why Englishmen were so much better dressed than Frenchmen, he replied laconically, ' 'Tis the hat'" (Florence Howe Hall, *Social Customs* (Boston: Estes and Lauriat, 1887), p. 251).

## 111: "Wherever his wandering brought him"

With this explicit reference to the white stage

of the threefold martyrdom in the *Cambrai Homily*, Connolly depicts Blue as having accepted total abandonment to God's will through Lady Poverty. See the note "a better insight" under Chapter 3.

## 111: "Shiftless"

Blue's Incarnational desire to live among those considered indolent and ineffective stands in stark contrast to how Gatsby views his own father and mother: "His parents were shiftless and unsuccessful farm people—his imagination had never really accepted them as his parents at all" (*GG*, p. 104). A couple sentences earlier, James Gatz—Gatsby's real name—is described as a loafer, an identity to be discarded. Blue sees the men he reaches out to as "not loafers," not because he invents new personae for them but because he sees "they have the stuff of saints" (p. 93).

## 111: "Novitiate"

The first stage of living in a religious community after having been formally accepted, the novitiate is usually two years or more, depending on the order. Blue is using the term informally, but readers may connect this moment to the narrator's earlier observation that Blue "seemed the man to start a new order himself" (p. 59).

## 112: "A mission establishment"

The closing words of the Latin Mass are usually *Ite missa est*: it is the dismissal, or, go forth. However, embedded in these words is the very character of Christian mission: what you have received here—Word and Eucharist—go and give to others. Blue is doing exactly that, just as his contemporary, the great missionary St. Katharine Drexel (1858–1955), was setting up schools for the poor and underprivileged of all ethnicities and races throughout the United States.

## 112: "I have two men for converts"

Chesterton highlights St. Francis's first followers, "the two men who have the credit, apparently, of having first perceived something of what was happening in the world of the soul" (*CW*, Vol. 2, p. 61). These were Bernard of Quintavalle, a wealthy noble and now a Servant of God, and Peter Cattani, a canon or clergyman of a church near Assisi.

## 112: "Providence"

In a simple sense the means by which God always provides (*Deus providebit*), Providence refers more deeply to the doctrine by which we understand how God sustains, governs, and cares for the world while allowing free will and drawing all men to Himself. Since Blue speaks of the men's "new courage," his use of Providence suggests the context of total abandonment: no matter what one's state or condition in life, God arranges the present moment such that we can always grow in love of Him and our neighbor in cooperative response to His grace. The enduring book detailing this spirituality—*Abandonment to Divine Providence* by Fr. Jean-Pierre de Caussade, S.J.—was published in 1861, though its contents were much older.

## 112: "Derelicts"

Quite simply, "a person abandoned or forsaken" (*OED*); a homeless person. Any negative nuance would be the result of confusing the neutral meaning used here with the distinct connotation of the adjective, such as derelict in one's duties.

## 112: "Ill-fits"

This rare usage, especially in noun form, suggests an intended distinction from the closest likely word: misfits. Perhaps Connolly meant to avoid the negative connotation of "misfit" and emphasize Blue's positive view that each person he seeks is merely "unsuited or ill-suited to his or her environment, work, etc." (*OED*).

## 112: "Wastrels"

In this context, wastrel means "a good-for-nothing, idle, worthless, disreputable person." The word had gone out of use by the 1880s and seems to have been used exclusively by British writers (*OED*).

## 113: "Spies of God"

Because the narrator repeats this phrase several times, including in the last sentences of the book, it is of particular interest. Connolly may have been inspired by prolific Irish poet and novelist Katharine Tynan (1861–1931), whose "Any Wife" appeared in 1914's *Irish Poems*. The opening six lines read:

> *Nobody knows but you and I, my dear,*
> *And the stars, the spies of God, that lean and peer,*
> *Those nights when you and I in a narrow strait*
> *Were under the whips of God and desolate.*
> *In extreme pain, in uttermost agony.*
> *We bore the cross for each other, you and I.*

A spy of God in Connolly's time, Blessed Miguel Pro, S.J. (1891–1927) spent the last year and a half of his life offering the sacraments to the people of Mexico City in secret using elaborate disguises; Catholics were routinely hunted down and brutally killed. Fr. Pro was eventually caught and condemned to death on false charges. After forgiving his executioners, he shouted the cry of the Cristeros, "Viva Cristo Rey!" as he was shot. The Knights of Columbus magazine *Columbia*, of which Connolly was editor from 1924–1928, was banned by the Mexican government—along with the Knights—for speaking out boldly against the atrocities being committed there (Alton Pelowski, "Remembering Mr. Blue," *Columbia*, June 1, 2014).

## 113: "Desire for truth…affection for beauty"

In speaking of truth and beauty Blue refers to some of the classical Transcendentals of metaphysics: being itself; the good, true, and beautiful; the one. Both Aquinas and Suárez (see the note on "Xavier" under Chapter 4) have much to say on the Transcendentals. Blue's point is that common "crafts" can be sanctified through the reasonable witness of his "Spies" to truth and beauty.

## 113: "Its small whisper"

Not the "still small voice" (1 Kings 19:12 [*KJV*]) Elijah hears at the approach of the Lord, this speaker suggests weakness, anxiety, and mediocrity as answers to a spiritual undertaking. Such spiritual desolations, says St. Ignatius, are hallmarks of the enemy of human nature, whether the source be the world, the flesh, or the devil (see that note under Chapter 3).

## 114: "No place to lay their heads"

The narrator is quoting Christ: "The foxes have holes, and the birds of the air nests; but the Son of man hath not where to lay his head" (Luke 9:58).

## 115: "Mendicants"

In common use, a friar or Franciscan living on the charity of others. More precisely, "a member of any of the Christian religious orders whose members originally lived solely on alms" (*OED*).

## 115: "Fifty million"

Adjusted for inflation using the Consumer Price Index, that amount would be about $700 million in 2015.

## 115: "My vocation…very noble"

Blue gives the narrator the charitable benefit of the doubt: he is amassing a fortune in order to give it away. This intention echoes Chesterton's view of the heroic motives of St. Francis's first two followers: "a priest who rent his robes like the Publican and not like a Pharisee and a rich man who went away joyful, for he had no possessions" (*CW*, Vol. 2, p. 62).

## 116: "Boston City Hospital"

"The question of establishing a hospital for the worthy poor who are citizens of Boston was, at various times, agitated" (David W. Cheever et al., eds., *A History of the Boston City Hospital* (Boston: Municipal Printing Office, 1906), p. 1). The need was met with the opening of the Boston City Hospital in 1864 in the South End neighborhood, just north of Roxbury and south of Back Bay. Now the Boston Medical Center, the hospital continues to meet the needs of those they call the "underserved," who comprise about three-quarters of their patients.

## 117: "A sort of lark"

"A frolicsome adventure, a spree" (*OED*).

## 118: "Matt Talbot"

Declared Servant of God in 1947 and Venerable in 1975, Matt Talbot (1856–1925) was a lifelong resident of Dublin, Ireland, and overcame more than two decades of severe alcoholism in his conversion. Less than a year after his death, "a pamphlet telling of his life came to be written...

Within a few months 120,000 copies were sold" (Edward Duff, S.J., "Saint in Overalls," *The Irish Monthly* 68:807 (September 1940), p. 492).

A Franciscan Tertiary or member of the Third Order, Talbot indeed worked in a lumberyard and was greatly admired for his generosity to the poor. He is the unofficial patron of those suffering addictions.

## 119: "No rubbers"

"Overshoes or galoshes made of rubber" (*OED*).

## 120: "Dover and Washington Streets"

The narrator's description of this intersection as "particularly sordid" is no exaggeration. "By the end of the Great Depression, when homelessness reached a peak, virtually every major city had laid claim to a skid row district. In Boston, it became Dover Street" (Padraig O'Malley, ed., *New England Journal of Public Policy Special Issue: Homelessness* (Amherst: University of Massachusetts Press, 1992), p. 358). The intersection is about a mile northeast of the Boston City Hospital.

## 120: "Foot and hand brakes"

Braking technology developed rapidly in the early twentieth century, with the first four-wheel braking systems making their appearances in the early 1920s. Still, to stop fast-traveling cars quickly, one would need to apply both brakes, such as Tom Buchanan does when pulling into Wilson's gas station: "Tom threw on both brakes impatiently and we slid to an abrupt dusty stop under Wilson's sign" (*GG*, p. 129).

## 122: "The price of a pint of gin"

Joe has sacrificed, as it were, his nightly liquor money in order to buy a book for Blue. Redemptive suffering can be seen in how Blue, the one on the sickbed, actually heals those who come to him. One wonders if Connolly had somehow heard of Marthe Robin, a stigmatist and mystic who had become completely bedridden and paralyzed by 1927.

## 123: "His cot was empty"

Given the final paragraph of the book, it's hard not to hear Connolly setting up the "empty tomb" of the Resurrection for us in this line.

## 123: "Embolus"

Blue dies of an embolus, a mass like a blood clot that causes an embolism, "an obstruction in a blood vessel" (*OED*). With this plot twist—after all, Blue was expected to be released from the hospital—Connolly has brought Blue to the Red stage of the threefold martyrdom: total self-gift to the poorest of the poor, even unto death.

This is one of Connolly's keener wordplays, for the embolism is also a prayer of the Latin Mass (retained, yet slightly changed, in the Ordinary Form) said by the priest directly after everyone prays the Our Father. The embolism begins, "Libera nos, quaesumus, Domine…" The embolism beseeches God to deliver, through the secret prayer of the priest, everyone from all evil; invokes Mary, Mother of God; and asks for all this through Christ the Lord. See *CE*, "Libera Nos."

## 124: "Why should I be here"

Many Saints throughout history have asked the same question. For instance, a young Karol Wojtyła, who would become St. John Paul II, watched fellow seminarians simply disappear in WWII Kraków. "'So many young people of my own age are losing their lives, *why not me*?'" (Weigel, *Letters to a Young Catholic*, p. 171).

## 125: "Scott Jackson"

This reference is obscure. Given that everyone else in the list is more or less anonymous, perhaps the narrator's point is that the "wealthiest man in the state" is someone no one has heard of.

## 125: "You can't make me"

The narrator echoes the provocative saying of St. John Eudes (1601–1680): "Do you not know that only the thoughtless and insane consider the faithful departed to be dead?" (*Letters and Shorter Works*, trans. Ruth Hauser (New York: P. J. Kenedy & Sons, 1948), p. 9). St. John Eudes had a deep devotion to the Sacred Hearts of Jesus and Mary (see the note on "his heart bled" under Chapter 3). He was canonized in 1925 in the same ceremony with St. John Vianney.

The narrator, who has spent most of the book skeptical of Blue and silently disagreeing with him, has now become his most outspoken advocate.

Made in the USA
Middletown, DE
06 May 2021

39099901R00137